AF482947

Ray Bradbury, Henry Hasse, Antony Corvais...

Futuria Fantasia
(Vol.1-4)

e-artnow 2020

Authors

Ray Bradbury
Henry Hasse
Antony Corvais
Guy Amory
Erick Freyor
Emil Petaja
E.T. Pine
Ross Rockylyn
Lyle Monroe
J.E. Kelleam
Hank Kuttner
J.H. Haggard
Ron Reynolds
Damon Knight
Hannes V. Bok

Contents

Futuria Fantasia I

Greetings! At Long Last-Futuria Fantasia!

The best laid plans of men, it seems, are destined for detours or permanent and disappointing annihilation upon the road to accomplishment. It was this way with Futuria Fantasia, planned for publication last summer. Piles of archaic tomes towered on all sides of the editorial desk. When the door to the office was opened unexpectedly a white gusher of manuscripts and relatives spewed out. More than once Ye Editor was suffocated unto death by the musty volumes that poured in from all over Los Angeles. And then-someone turned off the financial faucet-leaving us all soaped up, but with no water! And so, into an inforced hibernation went FuFa. The manuscripts became intimate acquaintances with all of the spiders in the family vaults-even the writers could be seen lounging around in their caskets waiting for Technocracy and their thirty doubloons every Thursday to come rolling in.

But recently, awakening from the profound inactivity of spring fever, your editor became interested in Technocracy. The more he heard about it, the more he wanted everyone else to hear. So, turning the revolving door on his crypt, he reached over and shook T. B. Yerke out of his stupor and begged him to write an article, The Revolt Of The Scientists, which appears herein. Not content with this he engaged Ron Reynolds, new fan author who first appeared in Tucker's D'JOURNAL, to whip up a story about the Technate and its effect upon the hack writer in the coming decades. And Ackerman is here! Science Fiction's finest fan and friend has turned in an interesting yarn that he wrote at the gentle age of sixteen, some few years past. But best of all-there is nothing humorous in the issue by the editor himself-which should cause huge, grateful sighs of relief from Maine to Miske and back! Bradbury just has a poem, and a serious one at that.

And so-here it is, for ten cents, out every other decade or so-Futuria Fantasia —...hypoed into Life mainly because of the crying need for more staunch Technocrats, mainly because of the New York Convention, (with which it doesn't deal at all in subject matter ...but does so whole-heartedly in spirit and thought), and mainly because it's been a helluva long time since a large size mag came from our LASFL way, where the natives are all sitting around and dreaming of the New York Canyon Kiddies and praying, atheistically of course, that in the near future they may wind up in Manhatten behind the pool-ball-perisphere —and I don't mean the one numbered *eight*. None of the expectant tripsters have ever seen New Yawk before and have already chewed their fingernails down to the shoulder in exstatic anticipation.

I hope you like this brain-child, spawned from the womb of a year long inanimation. If you do like it, how about a letter sent to the editorial offices of F.F., at 1841 South Manhatten Place, Los Angeles, California? Appoint yourself as A-1 mourner and critic and pound away at the mag. It will be appreciated. And if you have a dime in your pocket that hasn't had a breath of air in a few days just drop that in, too. This is only the first issue of FuFa ...if it succeeds there will be more, better issues coming up. And your co-operation is needed.

GOOD LUCK TO THE NEW YORK SCIENTI-FAN CONVENTION —!!

I'LL MEET YOU IN MANHATTEN —!

Ray D. Bradbury,

editor

The Revolt of the Scientists
by Technocrat Bruce Yerke

The editor of this magazine has asked me to prepare an article about a certain subject that has hitherto been totally lacking from the pages of all the scientifictional magazines, and which, with an article in a special LASFL publication, burst a bombshell on the science-fictional field, and at the same moment punched an irreparable hole in the Wollheim-Michel gas bag. Being recognized as the *science-fiction Technocrat*, I was asked to do this by Mr. Bradbury, who is himself a new recruit to OUR ranks. Since many of the readers of this magazine have all read the article in the first *MIKROS*, I feel that I can take a few liberties to go ahead.

When you write an introductory article to a generally new audience on Technocracy, you have to start from the ground up. You cannot assume that the readers know a whit about it. This, eventually, becomes boring to the *teacher*, for he is so exuberant and anxious to take up other phases of the subject that he soon gets tired of merely telling of the first stepping stone in a vast subject.

This article will cause much interrogation. It would be impossible for me, in this limited space, to give you all of the facts I wish to, but I do suggest that everyone who is interested should go to the nearest TECHNOCRACY INC. section (and there are many in every large city) and receive some of their literature, or write to CONTINENTAL HEADQUARTERS if you live at some flag stop, and get their pamphlets.

If you have ever heard of Technocracy, it was probably through some garbled news item, and thus you, like I myself, no doubt have or had a very wrong opinion of this organization. It is perfectly legal in all respects, being incorporated under the laws of New York State. It is technically an educational organization, and many authorities have to admit that Tech's twenty week study course is the equivalent of a 4 year college experience. The fact that its speakers are allowed to talk in public high schools, and hold meetings in the same place, shows that even the carefully censured school board is, at least, not opposing it.

Technocracy is not an organization that wants to overthrow the American government, but only an org. that will step in when the present Price System collapses. (At this point it MUST be taken note of that PRICE SYSTEM is not a different word for the Marxian definition of CAPITALISM. *Price SYSTEM* is merely a term designating *any system using a* circulating medium of exchange for the distribution of goods and services.)

If you go to a Technocracy section, they will show you a chart that will convince you that this *system* will collapse before 1945, probably 1942. This chart shows the economic trends of this nation from its birth to 1939, and also the amount of extraneous energy and human toil required to produce and maintain this economy. When you leave, you'll be convinced, don't worry. I have not the time nor space to do that here. The end of the Price System is inevitable, and when it comes you are not faced with the choice of taking Technocracy or Socialism, Communism or any other 'ism'. You are faced with a choice of Tech. or *chaos*, out of which the majority of us will not emerge-alive.

This nation is so highly inter-dependant, that the failure of one phase of its industrial sequence would mean the ultimate collapse of the whole country. If the electric power of New York was shut off, the city would burn down in approximately SIX HOURS! This, because of the rate fires break out. If the transportation system were shut off, all of the food in the city would be gone in six days, water would be so polluted that disease 10,000 times worse than the Black Plague would break out.

I shall not spend time telling you why we are faced with economic disaster, for thousands of examples can be had at a Technocracy section. We shall, for the purposes of this article simply assume that the collapse is near, within a matter of days.

All of the large business institutes, and Technocracy as well, will know within 100 days of the time of the ultimate end, when all stocks and bonds depreciate to zero and the financial structure of this country is due to fall.

At this time Technocracy will do, what is termed in colloquial American slang —"TURN ON THE HEAT!" At the present time Technocracy is not interested in forming a large organization, formed of emotional butterflys. It is constructing a functional group; a nucleus of people who know the subject to a T, and who will be prepared to act in the forming of a skeleton control until things are reorganized. In the last five years Technocracy has not used one bit of emotional fly paper, but has presented its whole plan in plain facts, and in as hard-boiled and unentertaining a manner as could be done without insulting the listeners. Nevertheless Tech. is the fastest growing organization in the nation. (except the relief organization)

Under Technocracy people will be classified in a set of probably 100 industrial sequences, according to their work. Each of these is known as a FUNCTIONAL SEQUENCE. Let us trace the work of one sequence from the bottom to the top.

The nation will be divided into regional divisions, determined by latitude and longitude. In each division there will be the various offices of whatever sequences are operating in that division. (each sequence of the 100 different ones will not necessarily appear in every division, though) Some will only have three or four or even as high as fifty. In this division we will find, say, a factory, for the production of steel, and thus there will be a steel sequence in this division. (This is how it will work in all sequences, essentially.)

The lowest classification will be the man doing the simplest job. We'll use as our example one who works a welding torch. All the welding torch workers in that factory will be under a foreman. He will be elected out of the torch workers as the one most efficient, working the best, who is most popular, though the latter factor's not so influencing as it is at present.

All the foremen in that area division will elect a divisional head of foremen of torch welding crews. Out of all the head foremen of torch and steel dumping crews and the other numerous distinct functions, there will be elected a division head. The division heads then elect a national head. The national heads of all the other sequences will form what will be known as the Continental Control, electing an executive director, merely a presiding officer, with not even the powers of the present president. He is answerable to, not answered to.

All the other basic functions will have essentially the same organization, and it is anticipated there will 90 to 110 of them. At the present time 93 have been worked out. The one thing of note is that there will not be more than FOUR offices between Armando Pinccio of the garbage truck crew and the head of the national sequence of waste disposal.

The thing of most interest to all interested is the method of purchase or what is referred to as the MEDIUM OF EXCHANGE. In the TECH THERE IS NO MEDIUM OF EXCHANGE, THERE IS ONLY A METHOD OF TECHNOLOGICAL ACCOUNTING.

The means whereby you will get a new razor blade or a malted milk is to be known as DISTRIBUTION CERTIFICATES or ENERGY CERTIFICATES. These certificates, issued to every person on this continent every 30 days, will be good only for one person and no other. Since they will be able to purchase as much or, I should say, since they will give the individual purchasing power of 20,000 dollars per year, each will have everything he needs. Stop right now and think what this means in the reduction of crime. These certificates cannot be stolen, and since every one will have all they can possibly use, there will be no need to steal.

With the technological development on this continent at present it is possible to turn out, at peak production, enough for every person to have a terrific abundance, and to do this, with a little mechanization done in the period of a month or so, it is only necessary for every able individual male, twixt ages 25 & 45, to work fours hours a day, 4 days a week, for 165 days a year-to keep this production turning over. If any one works more, someone else works less. So draw your own conclusions.

All things under the TECHNATE will be controlled, numbered by a modified DEWEY DECIMAL SYSTEM, as used in libraries now. The energy certificate will have on its face the sex, age, job, place of birth, address, where he works, and the worker's number, all recorded by this system. There are also places for purchases, four, to be exact. When one makes up his mind to buy something, he goes to the store (an example) and buys a pair of shoes. By means of a photoelectric machine (already developed) the salesclerk would punch out numbers and the certificate would come out bearing, neatly perforated: "34.46...11.E.728.../..H76302../...Z.97321.../...205...21.05." All this means that the article was a pair of low shoes, made by the leather sequence, that they were men's shoes, width E, last number 7, and style 8. Second series of numerals are the serial numbers of the machine, third is the number of certificate, the last the date and time.

At the end of the day the total lever of the machine would be pressed, and all the numbers, styles, etc. would be separated into totals (like nickels and dimes in a coin changing machine). The totals would then be teletyped to the divisional H.Q. of the leather sequence where it would be registered. This affords a continuous inventory of the whole continent. The following day, as many shoes as had been sold in the continent would be manufactured.

Many things, such as housing, transportation, medical care, recreation, education, etc. are furnished by Technocracy. One can easily see what a secure life this affords every citizen, and what a boon it is to scientific research.

I said that I wouldn't mention many things that would solve questions in the reader's minds, but if all questions are sent to the editorial offices we will contrive to open a forum.

In closing remember these few things. Technocracy is NOT a political or revolutionary movement. It is 100% American. It cannot work anywhere but on the American continent, because only here have we the necessary technological developements, the necessary trained force of technicians, and the necessary resources to institute an economy of abundance in place of an economy of scarcity. Technocracy is the only salvation when the Price System fails. It is not a political theory, but the next state of civilization. It is the best form of democracy ever conceived. It furnishes security, education, protection, and all that goes, with it to the people of the American continent. It is not in its formative state. It could be installed on a seventy-two hour call. The only reason why we don't have it now is because YOU are still duped to believing there is another way out.

Take Technocracy, or take — —chaos!

Don't Get Technatal
by Ron Reynolds

For several moments Stern had eyed his typewriter ominously, contemplating whether he should utter the unutterable. Finally:

"Damn!" he roared. "I can't write any more! Look, look at that!" He tore the sheet out of the rollers and crumpled it in his fist. "If I'd known it would be this way," he said, "I wouldn't have voted for it! Technocracy is ruining everything!"

Bella Stern, preoccupied with her knitting, glanced up in horror. "What a temper," she exclaimed. "Can't you keep your voice down?" She fussed with her work. "There now," she cried, "you made me drop a stitch!"

"I want to be a writer!" Samuel Stern lamented, turning with grim eyes to his wife. "And the Technate has spoiled my fun."

"The way you talk, Samuel," said his wife, "I actually believe you want to go back to that barbarism prevalent in the DARK THIRTIES!"

"It sounds like one damned good idea!" he said. "At least I'd have something decent, or indecent, to write about!"

"What *can* you mean?" she asked, tilting her head back and thinking. "Why can't you write? There are just oodles of things I can think of that are readable."

Something like a tear rolled down Samuel's cheek. "No more gangsters, no more bank robberies, no more holdups, no more good, old-fashioned burglaries, no more vice gangs!" His voice grew lachrymose as he proceeded down an infinite line of 'no mores'. "No more sadness," he almost sobbed. "Everybody's happy, contented. No more strife and hard work. Oh, for the days when a gangland massacre was headline scoop for me!"

"Tush!" sniffed Bella. "Have you been drinking again, Samuel?"

He hiccoughed gently.

"I thought so," she said.

"I had to do something," he declared. "I'm going nuts for want of a plot."

Bella Stern laid her knitting aside and walked to the balcony, looked meditatively down into the yawning canyon of the New York street fifty stories below. She turned back to Sam with a reminiscent smile.

"Why not write a love story?"

"*WHAT!*" Stern shot out of his chair like a hooked eel.

"Why, yes," she concluded. "A nice love story would be very enjoyable."

"LOVE!" Stern's voice was thick with sarcasm. "Why, we don't even have decent love these days. A man can't marry a woman for her money, and vice-versa. Everyone under Technocracy gets the same amount of credit. No more Reno, no more alimony, no more breach of promise, or law suits! Everything is cut and dried. The days of society weddings and coming out parties are gone-cause everyone is equal. I can't write political criticisms about graft in the government, about slums and terrible living conditions, about poor starving mothers and their babies. Everything is okay-okay-okay —" his voice sobbed off into silence.

"Which should make you very happy," countered his wife.

"Which makes me very sick," growled Samuel Stern. "Look, Bell, all my life I wanted to be a writer. Okay. I'm writing for the pulp magazines for a coupla years. Right? Okay. Then I'm writing sea stories, gangsters, political views, first class-bump-offs. I'm happy....I'm in my element. Then-bingo! —in comes Technocracy, makes everyone happy-bump! out goes me! I just can't stand writing the stuff the people read today. Everything is science and education." He ruffled his thick black hair with his fingers and glared.

"You should be joyful that the population is at work doing what they want to do," Bella beamed.

Sam continued muttering to himself. "They took all the sex magazines off the market first thing, all of the gangster, murder and detective publications. They been educating the children and making model citizens out of them."

"Which is as it should be," finished Bella.

"Do you realize," he blazed, whipping his finger at her, "that for two years there hasn't been more than a dozen murders in the city? Not one suicide or gang war-or —"

"Heavens!" sighed Bella. "Don't be prehistoric, Sam. There hasn't been anything really criminal for twenty years now. This is 1975 you know." She came over and patted him gently on the shoulder. "Why don't you write something science-fictional?"

"I don't like science," he spat.

"Then your only alternative is love," she declared firmly.

He formed the despicable word with his lips, then: "No, I want something new and different." He got up and strode to the window. In the penthouse below he saw half a dozen robots moving about speedily, working. His face lit up suddenly, like that of a tiger spying his prey. "Jumping Jigwheels!" he cried. "Why didn't I think of it before! Robots! I'll write a love story about two robots."

Bella squelched him. "Be sensible," she said.

"It might happen some day," he argued. "Just think. Love oiled, welded, built of metal, wired for sound!" He laughed triumphantly, but it was a low laugh, a strange little sound. Bella expected him to beat his chest next. "Robots fall in love at first sight," he announced, "and blow an audio tube!"

Bella smiled tolerantly. "You're such a child, Sam, I sometimes wonder why I married you."

Stern sank down, burning slowly, a crimson flush rising in his face. Only half a dozen murders in two years, he thought. No more politics, no more to write about. He had to have a story, just had to have one. He'd go crazy if something didn't happen soon. His brain was clicking furiously. A calliope of thought was tooting in his subconscious. He had to have a story. He turned and looked at his wife, Bella, who stood watching the air traffic go by the window, bending over the sill, looking down into the street fifty floors below....

...and then he reached slowly and quietly for his atomic gun.

AN EXPLANATION: You may have wondered why I placed the Technocrat story and article in FuFa. Well, it's because I think Technocracy combines all of the hopes and dreams of science-fiction. We've been dreaming about it for years-now, in a short time it may become reality. It surely deserves support from any serious fictioneer. And you can't say this mag isn't balanced! —first I give you Yorke's article on Tech., then I give you a satire on the same thing, jabbing at it in a good-humoured way, and then-when you read Ackerman's article, you'll see almost the complete annihilation of EARTH. So, whether you are an optimist or a pessimist about the future of humanity, you'll find either side in FuFa. (But on the side, I'm all for the Technate, aegh!)

Ye Editor....

This being the first issue of FuFa I feel fortunate in being able to offer a piece of scientifiction by the field's most famous fan.

THE RECORD was written first in 1929, scarcely more than a sketch, on two pages. Ackerman was thirteen. ED EARL REPP, LA author of THE RADIUM POOL, said of it: "I found it delighting and exceptionally interesting for the writing of a boy so young." Ackerman re-wrote it into a three page story, later, the present product. It has not been touched since. It is not being retouched now. Allow me to present THE RECORD as a *record* of how Forrie wrote, spelled and punctuated six years ago at the age of sixteen. *ED.*

The Record
by Forrest J. Ackerman

For twenty years-for twenty long, horror filled, war laden years the Earth had not known peace.

Hovering over the metropolises of the world came long, lean battle projectiles, glinting silver in the sunlight or coming like gaunt mirages of grey out of the midnight sky to blast man's civilization from its cultural foundations. Man against man, ship against ship —a ceaseless and useless orgy of slaughter. Men, at their battle stations in the ships, pressed buttons, releasing radio bombs that blistered space and lifted whole cities up in shattered pieces and flung them down, grim ruins, reminders of man's ignorant hatreds and suspicions.

And gas-thick black clouds of it-billowing over the cities, seeking every possible egress, pushed forward by colossal Wind machines. But even when Victory came for the one side, often Nature, in one of her vengeful moments, would send the black gas flowing back to annihilate its senders.

Rays cut the air! Power bombs exploded incessantly! Evaporays robbed the Earth of its water-shot it up into the atmosphere and made of it a fog that condensed only after many months. And heat rays made deserts out of fertile terrain.

Rays that hypnotized caused even the strong minded to commit suicide or reveal military secrets. Rays that effected the optical nerves swept cities and left the population groping and blind, unable to find food.

It was a war that destroyed almost all of humanity. And why were they fighting? *For pleasure and amusement!*

In the middle of the twenty-second century, every nation had a standard defense. The weapons of war of each were equal-not in proportion to size, but actually, since man-power no longer counted high. Pacifism had done its best, but the World was armed to the hilt. And now-though illogically-it felt safe-for every nation meant the same as if all had nothing.

Another thing-there was no work to be done. Robots did it. And there seemed nothing left to discover, invent or enjoy. Art was at its perfection, poetry was mathematically correct and unutterably beautiful-worked out by the Esthetic machines. Sculptoring had been given the effect complete, artists hands guided by wonderful pieces of machinery. Huge museums were crammed with art put out synthetically.

And thus it was with the many Arts and their creators who grew stagnent in their perfection. And it was that way with the many sciences also....

Paleontologists had found, and articulated, and catalogued every fossil. The ancestor of the Eohippus, the little four-toed Dawn Horse, was discovered; the direct line between man and ape established in skeletal remains; the seat of *life* itself definitely proved Holarctica. And great bio-chemists, skilled in the science of vital processes, had created synthetic tissues and muscles and flesh, built upon the frames that had been recovered bodies with skillful modeling ... even supplied them with blood and given them the spark of LIFE ... so that Paleobotonists recreated the flora of a prehistoric era. Again the ponderous amphibious brontosaur pushed through marshes. Fish emerged upon the land, and the first bird archaeopteryx tried his imperfect wings for flight. In the regulated climates of long dead ages, fish, amphibians, reptiles, birds and mammals lived again for the edification of those interested in the very ancient-or who were amused with queer animals.

But that was only paleontologically speaking. There were the heavens to be considered. They had been: the stars and planets weighed and measured, their composition noted, courses plotted with super-accuracy. Every feature had been mapped-every climactic condition recorded. Life had been named and numbered ...then photographed. And these were but first considerations. Actually, what wasn't known about the Solar System had not occurred as yet. But that would probably be remedied by a machine to view the future.

There was physics, biology, anthropology, zoology, geology, bacteriology, botany-and 'olo-gies' and 'otonies' and 'onomies' such as ran into figures which only machines could calculate.

A book could indeed have been written of the accomplishments of super race. But this is of the WAR itself, and how it came about, and how it all ended.

Stated simply, in 2150 the point of DIMINISHING UTILITY had been reached. To the hungry man, the first course of dinner is wonderfully delicious, the second good, the third satisfying. Through the ages people have hungered after luxury and leisure-but when he finds his food, a lot of it, MAN finds suddenly that it no longer appeals to him. In fact, too much is bound to make him sick and often disagreeable. He looks around for something else. So did the people of the 22nd Century. They had all of the pleasurable amusements they wanted, but it was all so intellectual. Everything was culture. They had surfeited with it. And suddenly they wanted to forget it. All play and no work made MAN a discontented citizen. A reaction set in. Man was not completely civilized as yet — —THE WAR!

Twenty-one years the war raged. And scarcely a million survived. Bit by bit this million was whittled down by the weapons of destruction to ragged handfuls of things that once had been cultured. Finally only one hundred humans remained alive-and they kept fighting blindly, none of them realizing how close to oblivion they were crowding themselves and the future of humanity-and they went on killing, killing, killing!

It is doubtless but what the entire human race would have vanished, leaving the world to the more competent, though half-ignorant, hands of the beasts, who fought and killed one another for self-preservation and for food-not because of madness ... and who did not have books and talk and have *culture*. The human race would have gone, had it not been for the record.

The fighters of WAR'S END, leaving their machines and countries to congregate for personal combat, were engaging in hand-to-hand attacks in the ruins of what once had been a tall and powerful city in the Twentieth Century, but now lay crumbling, its proud buildings falling to the ground, sticking out iron-rusted skeletons to the sky-and the city was LOS ANGELES!

HEDRIK HUNSON was fighting with phosphorized fists-hand inclosed in chemically treated gloves that burned as they struck the antagonist, insulated on the interior for the wearer-when suddenly the two of them were caught by a spreader. The other man died instantly, but Hedrik got it in the side and was whirled about sickeningly, and survived.

He was lying painfully on something when he came to, but felt too dizzy and sick to move. At last, when his head had cleared a bit, he rolled over into a sitting position and reached out his arms to grasp —a phonograph!

Big things came in small packages in the days of 2171, and a portable phonograph might well be taken for a weapon of some sort-which was exactly what Hedrik thought! And you can hardly blame him, because no one in that generation had ever seen one of the things.

There was a curious story connected with the dying of music, concerning the days of 2050 when there was a movement to stamp out all symphonies and songs and things even slightly sentimental.

—but back to Hedrik!

Hedrik found the crank that wound the portable, turned it, reasoning that perhaps it gave power-and then-holding it away from him-he waited for rays to spurt out or something to explode. Nothing happened! Hedrik was disappointed. After an agony of perspiration and puzzlement he finally accidentally placed the needled arm onto the disk. The disk, he noticed, was black and filled with little undulations. The disk was like a wheel-so Hedrik thought-it should revolve like one, shouldn't it? He pushed the starter thoughtfully and was more than surprised when the disk started spinning.

From the phonograph came music-music and singing! The lost Art had returned! The Art banished under compulsion had made a comeback.

Some man was singing on the record-in a queerly interesting and familiar tongue, the ancient English. The singer seemed sad, almost crying. And Hedrik was thrilled as he played it over and over again, drinking in the new experience like wine on the lips of a connoisseur. The voice rose, fell, lingered. And Hedrik suddenly didn't feel like fighting anymore!

The music floated out over the tumbled ruins, descended to the ears of the other people. AND THE FIGHTING CEASED! They were transformed. They came running to crowd about the machine.

And there in that aged music shop they stood enthralled-music filled their souls. It was exactly what they had needed and wanted for many years. And it had been denied them. Music was the balancing force ... the force that would help them struggle ahead rebuilding the world. And next time they would be saner ... they knew ... the lesson of luxury had been learned and learned well. Never again would they leave all of the work to the machines. Now they would work and sing and play.

It would be work ... hard work ... for some time to come. But they had found music again, and that would anchor them to sanity.

And thus was mankind saved through a record —*SONNY BOY!*

FUTURIA FANTASIA! FALL ISSUE COMING UP AS SOON AS YE EDITOR RE-TURNS FROM JAUNT TO MANHATTEN (in case you intend writing me and telling me I spelled MANHATTAN wrong in the editorial and above, I already know it ... it was just a typical-graphical error.) THE NEXT ISSUE WILL BE EVEN LARGER-CONTAINING YOUR COMMENTS ON FUFA AND ARTICLES BY ACKERMAN, YERKE, HENRY KUTTNER, JACK ERMAN AND RON REYNOLDS. There will also be a play by play dew-scription of the trip to New Yawk and the happenings there in the science-fiction outfield-by Bradbury of course.

Thought and Space
by Ray D. Bradbury

Space-thy boundaries are
Time and time alone.
No earth-born rocket,
seedling skyward sown,
Will ever reach your cold,
infinite end,
This power is not Man's to
build or send.
Great deities laugh down,
venting their mirth,
At struggling bipeds on
a cloud-wrapped Earth,
Chained solid on a war-swept,
waning globe,
For FATE, who witnesses,
to pry and probe.
BUT LIST! One weapon have
I stronger yet!
Prepare Infinity! And
Gods regret!
Thought, quick as light,
shall pierce the veil,
To reach the lost beginnings
Holy Grail.
Across the sullen void on
soundless trail,
Where new spawned suns and
chilling planets wail,
One thought shall travel
midst the gods' playthings,
Past cindered globes where
choking flame still sings.
No wall of force yet have ye
firmly wrought,
That chains the supreme
strength of purest thought.
Unleashed, without a body's
slacking hold,
Thought leaves the ancient
Earth behind to mold.
And when the galaxies have
heeded DEATH,
And welcomed lastly SPACE'S
poisoned breath,
Still shall thought travel
as an arrow flown.

FAMOUS LAST WORDS:

"But, Mr. Smith, how do you explain that gyro-statistic-electromagnetiosonomonator on the radiostuntomotor?"
  "CLUNK!"

Futuria Fantasia II

A newer, plumper Futuria Fantasia greets you, with more articles, more value and less Technocracy! The reason for the scanty garb of our summer issue was TIME, that villain who holds his sword over all humanity. I didn't have time to contact various authors and fans-and there was little time for mimeographing, since the Angel expedition to New York was fast approaching, and ye editor was wandering around in a daze waiting for the day when his bus would sweep him off to Manhattan. The trip to New York was a happily successful thing. Futuria Fantasia would like to toss an orchid to the editors who contributed so generously to the convention, and at the same time blare forth with a juicy razzberry for a certain trio of fans who made fools of themselves at the Conv. (and u know who we meen).

But enuf of this boring fan quarreling ** action should have been taken at the convention and there's no use bawling over fused rockets. This issue we bring you another cover by Hans Bok. We sincerely believe his work is superior to any work done in fan mags for a long time. He has to be good ** for he is a protegee of no less a person than Maxfield Parrish, whose paintings have, at one time or another in the past decades, made more than one home beautiful. If you haven't had a Maxfield Parrish painting in yur home, it ain't a home. And, we feel proud of Hans becuz we acted as agent to Weird Tales while conventioneering in New York. Latest report is that Hans is doing an Illustration for Weird Tales. Here's luck, Hans, and may you keep up the good work while staying in Manhattan.

With this issue we introduce two new fans, and two new authors. They are Anthony Corvais, who makes his part-time home in Tucson, Arizona, and Guy Amory of Phoenix. Corvais, twenty-two years old, has done a neat job with his RETURN FROM THE DEAD. In the winter edition he will let go with another original SYMPHONIC ABDUCTION. Guy Amory, after sum few hours of hard labor, finally got an interview out of Hankuttner, which is work in any man's lingo. Both boys were in L.A. for two weeks about a month back, and gave their promise to support FuFa from now to TDWACOH (the day when *astounding* comes out hourly).

Ron Reynolds, whose satire on Technocracy received favorable comment, comes back with his views and news about the Convention ** and Corrinne Ellsworth, gracious female fan of L.A. presents us with something that is distasteful to me, THE CASE OF THE VANISHING CAFETERIA. I protest against her grossly horrid insinuations about my Ghoul's Broths. Manhattaneers will tell you that it is only at the full moon that I can concoct one ...tho a cafeteria or Automat atmosphere does work wonders with my ego-specially if there are enuf people watching to make it profitable.

As you will notice there is not a great deal to be sed about Technocracy in this issue ** mainly becuz I am tired of talking and the response we get is vury, vury funny, if not childish. If someone cares to challenge us on Technocracy we shall be only too glad to answer all questions, but when a bunch of crackpots start dragging in their own theories, relatives and human nature then we give up the ghost. We take this occasion to challenge the so-far-silent John W. Campbell to a duel of words on this subject. How's about it, Campbell?

The Galapurred Forsendyke
A tale of the Indies-by H.V.B.

He remembered-but never dreamed its source-the old poem which began, "A swibosh is an Indian," and as he leaned back in his chair puffing on a pipe, his lean bronzed face darkly serious against the moonglow, a little echo hooted from the hills as if an owl'd cried.

Then Edris called. At the alarmant tingle of the bell, like a tinnient tang of a rattlesnake's tremor, he ran to the telephone and shouted eagerly, "Edris! My darling." Then he remembered to take receiver off the hook. He was answered by dead silence. Then, to his amazement and utter horror, a long damp tongue swished out of the mouthpiece, lapped his cheek and disappeared in a puff of acrid steam. "The Martians!" was his first thot, as he tremblingly buttered his toast. Then he heard Edris' voice. It floated easily from the ceiling as if it were inverted steam. He looked up, and discovered overhead that the planet India had vanished from the map. It had peeled itself loose and inched over the wallpaper and was now wrapping itself like a second skin around a baked potato. "But that's impossible!" he breathed, "There aren't any potatoes in August, and especially in bathtubs." Again Edris' voice reached him. What was she saying? "Go with the pretty men, dear, they'll feed you an orange." But that sounded crazy. He was worried, and clung to a red-hot radiator which melted into a puddle at his touch, burning a round red hole in the rug.

Seventeen puffs of black vapor-he counted them-whiffed up winsomely from the charred circle. "Around and around," he said, dreamily, remembering the second line of the poem, "When Fifthly is perplexed." Edris oozed out of the shadows to him, longlike and snaky, with fearthy fettles adorning her foresome, and a blaze in her eyes like the hurmwurst of Whidby. Island, island, he repeated to himself, thrusting an negatory hand thru the farthing of her wrabdy-and her mouth parted to disclose another mouth, from which issued visible words like ticker tape of steam in chilly air, so surprising him that he could only stand rooted, like a tree. It was then that he noticed the snakes in her hair, as the leaves sprouted from his cheeks end from every simple vascicle of his tubular perpendages sometimes cursorily applellated, eyebreams.

Among the amiderie of her fascinating fingers, which she waved before his face like the shimmer of phosphorescence on a salty sea on hot midsummer moonlight, took shape an elegant form, something reminiscent of a redchief. Within his sore heart a black thot grew, spurred by the excess of his agonized birdtwitters, bidding him to slay and do so quickly. He reached for a weapon. There was nothing at hand but a slug. He groaned. A slug against snakes? What chance of victory? As tho she'd read his thot, she moved nearer, her laffter lifting and lowering like a fragile boat on waves of honey. One by one her eyes —390 of them-popped out with hollow slaps like corks from bottles, while within the dull draperies of scarlet which adorned the farthest lamp-post stirred an unnameable bloody something which sent forth a thrill of foreboding into his anguished heart, and he remembered the 4th and last lines of the poem "He who dines alone is hexed." He uttered a gurgling scream as she leaped upon him, and her snales torn and the steam of her bare eye-sockets scalded him-then the ensanguined thing crawled limply over the face of the blinding desert and the vacant sun stared sitelessly at nothing.

I'm Through!
by *Foo E Onya*

The editor of this magazine, under the impression that I am still one of that queer tribe known as science-fiction fans, has asked me to write an article. I am no longer a science-fiction fan. I'M THROUGH! However, I have decided to do the article and explain with my chin leading just why I am through. Here goes.

As to science-fiction; the trouble with me, I think, is that I have outgrown the stuff mentally-and that's not a boast, seeing the type of minds modern science-fiction is dished up for. I'll admit there are a few exceptions, but on the whole, s.f. fans are as arrogant, self-satisfied, conspicuously blind, and critically moronic a group as the good Lord has allowed to people the Earth. I don't blush that I was once a s.f. fan, starting back in '26 —I merely thank my personal gods that somewhere along the route I woke up and began to see s.f. as it really is. The superiority complex found in group known as science fiction fans is probably unequalled anywhere. Their certitude in their superiority, as readers of s.f., over all other fiction, is representative of an absolutely incredibly stupid complacence. Facing the business squarely, we can see why s.f. lays CLAIM to such superiority: for no other obvious reason than that such fiction is the bastard child of science and the romantic temperament. But NOT, good lord, because it is INSTRUCTIVE! This has too long been preached, until s.f. readers actually believe it! The amazing *naivette* of these readers who think their literature is superior merely because they think it teaches-this simple moves me to despair. The fact is, any literature whose function it is to teach, ceases to be literature *as such*; it becomes didactic literature, which is the color of another horse. When literature becomes obsessed by *ideas as such*, it is no longer literature. Just how the delusion could have arisen that writing, because invested with scientific symbols, automatically became possessed of new and more precious values, is beyond me to explain. Ideas are out of place in literature unless they are subordinate to the spirit of the story-but s.f. readers have never perceived this. "Give us SCIENCE!" they shriek, running with clenched fists uprisen to the stars. "We want SCIENCE! Give us the Great God!" Well, they are given *science*, and what does it turn out to be? For the most part the off-scourings of the lunatic fringe. Talk about scientists being inspired by s.f. stories-WHEW! Why, not one s.f. writer in fifty has the remotest idea of what he is talking about-he just picks up some elementary idea and kicks hell out of it. I'll wager that no scientist is going to produce very spectacularly on the basis of any ideas provided by s.f. It's possible, but wholly improbable. Scientists don't tick that way.

Another amusing fallacy: this well-known business of Wells and Verne doing some *predicting*. It's one of the biggest laffs of all. They made a *flock* of predictions, a few of which were realized, and some only in ways most vaguely related to the original conception. How many ideas did they have that *never* have been realized and never will? Give them credit for being good and often logical guessers, perhaps-but don't claim that as a merit for their WRITING! And how many other good guessers must there have been who never got around to setting down their predictions in print?

There is but one affectation about Wells' "scientific" stories which he published before he discovered his capability at characterization, and this is the affectation of imagination. There is no genuine imagination in beating out cleverness of the s.f. type; the point of view, the inventive quality necessary for their construction, is the same as with the widely circulated tales of Nick Carter. Science-fiction stories are not struck forth with a creative hand, they are manufactured products put together piece-meal —none of them being written in any but the calmest and most conscious mood. They are lacking in that important element of all really GREAT works of the imagination: inspiration. And what is inspiration? It is essentially the soaring of one's soul without the knowledge of the mind. In the gleaming moment the mind becomes the slave of the spirit. Read Wells' EXPERIMENT IN AUTOBIOGRAPHY and see why and what he thinks of his early writings of s.f. He admits that they were only a means to an end, a preparation for his more serious writing that was to come later-Plato's REPUBLIC and More's UTOPIA also serving largely to hasten Wells' Utopian proclivities. When he really began to take his predictions seriously, he began to turn out the important stuff which now bores the average s.f. enthusiast silly-or should I say sillier!

As for Verne, his stuff has never been literature except for boys. It is innocuous adventure-stuff that will not pervert morals. It is not too badly written, and the language is so simple that Verne is readily to be read in the original French, in fact some of his stuff serves as textbooks in French classes in American schools.

But in the main, what I am speaking about now is s.f. as it is constituted today. All of this modern s.f. is worthless except in perhaps *one minor respect*, and I'm not even sure of that. It CAN open the minds of boys and girls reaching puberty, giving them a more catholic attitude toward startling new ideas. However, it is so very often fatal at the same time, in that these boys and girls become obsessed with it-it enmeshes them until, as I said, they become incredibly blind to all else, so certain are they of the superiority of their hobby over all other fiction. There are exceptions, but my experience has proven that the exceptions are by far a minority.

Also I will admit that s.f. can on occasion provide escapist flights of imagination-in fact, it can be admirable for this; but this type of s.f. has become exceedingly rare because this crazy superstructure of SCIENCE, and even more so ADVENTURE, has become such a fetish that sound writing concerning people is rarely to be found. In pulp science-fiction, never.

And the frightful smugness fostered by the modern s.f. magazines is simply appalling. It seems that not only the readers, but the editors and writers as well, cannot or will not see anything beyond their own perverted models. Just as one example which I remember very well, look how BRAVE NEW WORLD, the admirable and really important novel by Huxley, was received a few years ago. It was Clark Ashton Smith, I believe, who mentioned it as embodying some of Huxley's "habitual pornography" —simply, stunning P. Schyler Miller; whom, I might mention, I consider as one of the most intellectual authors and fans. And, reviewing the book, C.A. Brandt also decried its preoccupation with sex, but said complacently that it might, at least, bring to the attention of people that there was such a thing as the science-fictionists and their so-called literature. Of all the damned nonsense! BRAVE NEW WORLD was, as a matter of fact, a satire on sex, and of FAR MORE IMPORTANCE than to "bring to the attention of people that there is such a thing as sci-fiction." Huxley conceived a future world in which Ford's mechanistic contributions had become so emphatic as to deprive the people of all but an animal interest in sex; he projects a more normal man into such a civilization for no other reason than to characterize present-day tendencies with searing satire. But Brandt-he evidently would demolish this to set up in its stead a "Space-wrecked On Mars" atrocity.

To get back to the subject, it is my honest opinion that no person of very conspicuous intelligence can subsist very considerably on s.f. after he begins to mature intellectually. There is simply not enuf *to* it to provide intellectual or spiritual nourishment. He may string along with it for a few years out of habit or some mental quirk-but stuff aimed at juvenile minds cannot very long sustain a person of mature years, unless that person is himself a mental adolescent. The way the fans flocked to the S.F. League, indulged in "tests" to prove their "superiority" over other readers, the silly letters in the mags, the petty internal strife, and many other things, have served to widen the gulf between me and s.f.

The most important thing, however, is that I have discovered that there's been too much else of importance, REAL importance, that has been said and written in this world (and is being and will be), for me to desire to give much attention to such a petty thing as s.f. any more. I shall read on the fringe of it, but increasingly less frequently I'm afraid.

I might have summed this entire thing up by saying, "I'm satiated," but that wouldn't be the entire truth. The entire truth would be: "I am satiated and much wiser." In conclusion let me point out that this is only one man's opinion. I have intentionally been harsh in my estimates, maybe some points are in need of qualification or elucidation, but by and large, I stand back of what I have written here. AMEN.

Satan's Mistress
by Doug Rogers

Where flames of purgatory twist, and Earth's transgressors dwell,
She dances swathed in heated mist, before the gates of Hell.
Her gleaming naked body flees before the Demon fires,
Along the shores of molten seas-ridged high by fuming pyres.
Her hair, a liquid cape of flame, whips hot about her breasts,
A strumpet in the Devil's name, which he alone invests,
Gives power to a woman born of brimstone, steam and smoke,
Her soul, a spark in early morn, flares up to share the yoke
Of evil Mephistopheles upon his throne of death,
Unheeding shrieks and doleful pleas choked out by dying breath.
The Devil's Mistress dances down thru dungeons carved from bone,
Upon her head the sinner's crown, each jewel a sigh, a moan.
Before the wailing souls in caves, tossed down from earthly things,
To charred and cindered minds of slaves her dancing passion brings.
Then, tired of her evil joke, and laughing at her games,

She draws about her fiery cloak to vanish in the flames.

Lost Soul
by Henry Hasse

From far across the desolate moor I heard
The echo of a wild and anguished cry —
A tortured voice that shrieked aloud a word,
A name, that shivered 'cross the leaden sky.
I stopped-stared 'round —I knew that voice did sound
A faint, familiar note within my brain.
I fled across that dark and desolate ground
Seeking out the direction whence it came.
Forebodingly, that voice kept echoing
Within a brain that did not seem my own...
A vague remembrance of a recent thing
I could not grasp ...I was a lost and lone
Forsaken soul that sped I knew not where,
Wondering frightenedly what I did seek....
At last I found it, there beside a bare
And lonely road, when trembling and weak,
I gazed upon a gallows-tree where hung
A corpse, the very site of which did freeze
The blood within my veins; a corpse that swung
Grotesquely to and fro upon the breeze.
And then, through rising panic, closer still
I peered-then saw! —and knew! Again that cry
That shrieked a name-the cry that issued shrill
From my own throat, and shivered to the sky!

* * * * *

The name I shriek beneath the gallows-tree

Was mine. The dead thing swinging there was me!

The Truth About Goldfish —
by Kuttner

For some time I have been wondering what the world is coming to. More than once I have got up in the middle of the nite, padded toward the bureau, and, peering into the mirror, exclaimed, "Stinky, what is the world coming to?" The responses I have thus obtained I am not at liberty to reveal; but I am coming to believe that either I have a most mysterious mirror or something is wrong somewhere. I am intrigued by my mirror.

It came into my possession under extraordinary and eerie circumstances, being borne into my bedroom one Midsummer's Eve by a procession of cats dressed oddly in bright-colored sunsuits and carrying parasols. I was asleep at the time, but awoke just as the last tail whisked out the door, and immediately I sprang out of bed and cut my left big toe rather badly on the edge of the mirror. I remember that as I first looked into the fathomless, glassy depths, a curious thot came into my mind. "What," I said to myself, "is the world coming to? And what is science-fiction coming to?"

It is quite evident that a logical and critical analysis of science-fictional trends is a desideratum today. The whole trouble, I feel, can be laid to velleity. (I have wanted to use that word for years. Unfortunately I have now forgotten exactly what it means, but one can safely attribute trouble to it. Where was I?)

Today science-fiction is split by schisms and impaled on the trylon of bad thots. The fans, I mean, not the writers. The writers have been split and impaled for years, but nothing can be done about that. In a way, it's a good thing. Look at Jules Verne, Victor Hugo, and, for that matter, the late unfortunate Tobias J. Koot.

I put flowers on his grave only yesterday. He lies at rest, tho his ghastly fate pursued him even to the grave. And I attribute Mr. Koot's fate to nothing less than the schisms of fandom. For Koot was a hard working young man, serious, earnest, with promise of becoming a first-class writer. He took life very solemnly-almost grimly. "My job," he told me once, "is to give people what they want."

"I want a drink," I said to him. "Give me one."

But Koot couldn't be turned from his rash course. He began to write science-fiction. That was where the trouble started. "Is it science?" he pondered. "Or is it fiction?" Already the cleavage-the split-had begun.

It was a matter of logical progression toward ultimate division. Koot got in the habit of typing the science into his stories with his left hand, and the fiction with his right. He began to twitch and worry. He got up nites. He was troubled, uneasy. "I have one thing left to cling to," he muttered desperately, "Fandom! I can point to that and say: It is real. It exists. It is dependable."

When fandom had its schism, Koot immediately developed a split personality. It was rather horrible. His left side-the scientific side-grew cold and hard and keen. He grew a Van Dyke on the left side of his face and his left hand was stained with acids and chemicals. But the right side of his face became dissipated and disreputable, with a leer in the eye end a scornful, sneering curve to the lip. He grew a tiny moustache on the right side, waxed it, and twirled it continually. It was rather horrid, but worse was yet to come.

One day the inevitable happened. Tobias J. Koot split in half, with a faint ripping sound and a despairing wail. He was, of course, buried in two coffins and in two graves, the wretched man's fate pursuing him even beyond death.

Well, you can understand how I feel, what with the mirror, the cats in sunsuits and the weasel. Or haven't I mentioned the weasel? I mean the brown one, of course, and he is, perhaps, worst of all. It isn't what he says so much as his sneering, ironic tone. The other weasels, who live in the spare bedroom with the colt, were happy enuf till HE arrived, but now THEY are arranging a schism. As you will readily see, something must be done about it before science-fiction collapses and the standard falls trailing into the dust.

I suggest that we mobilize, and, to avoid dissension, give everybody the rank of general. Then, first of all, we can march to my house and get rid of that weasel.

The Brown One, of course. The others are welcome to stay as long as they like. I feel that they are weak rather than wicked, and need only a good excuse, or should I say example, in order to brace themselves up.

Contributions to the fund for the mobilization of science-fiction and the extermination of brown weasels may be sent to me in care of this magazine. Do not delay. Each moment you wait brings us closer to doom, and, besides, I need a new piano.

H.K.

God Busters
by Erick Freyor

Mark Twain, in his *mysterious stranger*, makes no bones about his sentiments towards Christianity and the God illusion. Speaking of Christian progress he says, "It is a remarkable progress. In five or six thousand years five or six high civilizations have risen, flourished, commanded the wonder of the world, then faded out and disappeared; and not one of them except the latest ever invented any sweeping and adequate way to kill people. They all did their best-to kill being the chiefest ambition of the human race and the earliest incident in its history-but only the Christian civilization has scored a triumph to be proud of. Two or three centuries from now it will be recognized that all the competent killers are Christians; then the pagan world will go to school to the Christian, not to acquire his religion, but his guns. The *turk* and the *chinaman* will buy these to kill missionaries and converts with."

Again, in speaking of God, comparing the God conception to an impossible dream, he continues, "Strange, because they are so frankly and hysterically insane-like all dreams: a God who could have made good children as easily as bad, yet preferred to make bad ones; who could have made every one of them happy, yet never made a single happy one; who made them prize their bitter life, yet stingily cut it short; who gave his angels eternal happiness unearned, yet required his other children to earn it; who gave his angels painless lives, yet cursed his other children with biting miseries and maladies of mind and body; who mouths justice and invented hell-mouths mercy and invented hell; mouths Golden Rules and forgiveness multiplied by seventy times seven, and invented hell; who mouths morals to other people and has none himself; who frowns upon crimes, yet commits them all; who created man without invitation, then tries to shuffle the responsibility for man's acts upon man, instead of honorably placing it where it belongs, upon himself; and finally, with altogether divine obtuseness, invites this poor, abused slave to worship him!"

One wonders what the Christian Ethiopians thot when the Christian Italians playfully, and undoubtedly with the sanction of the Holy Mother Church, began to spray them with liquid fire, blast their cities, and mutilate their children with the newest Christian improvements on the Christian weapons of war. They probably couldn't quite understand the logic or the fairness of it, but we must not blame the Ethiopians for failing to comprehend, as they haven't had the benefits of Christian civilization for as long a time as the Italians.

Let's put a stop to this shilly-shallying. Let's put these destructive Atheists in their place. The Christians KNOW that God DOES exist. That God *is* all powerfull. So it would be only a simple matter to arrange an appointment with God, (we don't exactly know what his office hours are,) and prevail upon him to write a message in fire saying, "YOU BET, GOD IS THE REAL MCCOY" or something similar, and spread it all over the sky. That'll convince even the most reluctant Atheists, and it should be a rather simple trick for a God who once stopped the sun (sic!), created a universe in 6 days, and engineered an immaculate conception.

Clarence Darrow, world famous criminal lawyer, the man who made the Silver-Tongued and Godly Bryant appear the verbose addlepate he was, beneath his platitudinous phrases, during the Scopes trial, said, to an interviewer, "All my life I've been an Agnostic. But I am no longer an Agnostic, I am now an Atheist."

The Pendulum

Up and down, back and forth, up and down. First the quick flite skyward, gradually slowing, reaching the pinnacle of the curve, poising a moment, then flashing earthward again, faster and faster at a nauseating speed, reaching the bottom and hurtling aloft on the opposite side. Up and down. Back and forth. Up and down.

How long it had continued this way Layeville didn't know. It might have been millions of years he'd spent sitting here in the massive glass pendulum watching the world tip one way and another, up and down, dizzily before his eyes until they ached. Since first they had locked him in the pendulum's round glass head and set if swinging it had never stopped or changed. Continuous, monotonous movements over and above the ground. So huge was this pendulum that it shadowed one hundred feet or more with every majestic sweep of its gleaming shape, dangling from the metal intestines of the shining machine overhead. It took three or four seconds for it to traverse the one hundred feet one way, three or four seconds to come back.

THE PRISONER OF TIME! That's what they called him now! Now, fettered to the very machine he had planned and constructed. A pri-son-er-of-time! A —pris-on-er-of-Time! With every swing of the pendulum it echoed in his thoughts. For ever like this until he went insane. He tried to focus his eyes on the arching hotness of the earth as it swept past beneath him.

They had laughed at him a few days before. Or was it a week? A month? A year? He didn't know. This ceaseless pitching had filled him with an aching confusion. They had laughed at him when he said, some time before all this, he could bridge time gaps and travel into futurity. He had designed a huge machine to warp space, invited thirty of the worlds most gifted scientists to help him finish his colossal attempt to scratch the future wall of time.

The hour of the accident spun back to him now thru misted memory. The display of the time machine to the public. The exact moment when he stood on the platform with the thirty scientists and pulled the main switch! The scientists, all of them, blasted into ashes from wild electrical flames! Before the eyes of two million witnesses who had come to the laboratory or were tuned in by television at home! He had slain the world's greatest scientists!

He recalled the moment of shocked horror that followed. Something radically wrong had happened to the machine. He, Layeville, the inventor of the machine, had staggered backward, his clothes flaming and eating up about him. No time for explanations. Then he had collapsed in the blackness of pain and numbing defeat.

Swept to a hasty trial, Layeville faced jeering throngs calling out for his death. "Destroy the Time Machine!" they cried. "And destroy this MURDERER with it!"

Murderer! And he had tried to help humanity. This was his reward.

One man had leaped onto the tribunal platform at the trial, crying, "No! Don't destroy the machine! I have a better plan! A revenge for this-this man!" His finger pointed at Layeville where the inventor sat unshaven and haggard, his eyes failure glazed. "We shall rebuild his machine, take his precious metals, and put up a monument to his slaughtering! We'll put him on exhibition for life within his executioning device!" The crowd roared approval like thunder shaking the tribunal hall.

Then, pushing hands, days in prison, months. Finally, led forth into the hot sunshine, he was carried in a small rocket car to the center of the city. The shock of what he saw brought him back to reality. THEY had rebuilt his machine into a towering timepiece with a pendulum. He stumbled forward, urged on by thrusting hands, listening to the roar of thousands of voices damning him. Into the transparent pendulum head they pushed him and clamped it tight with weldings.

Then they set the pendulum swinging and stood back. Slowly, very slowly, it rocked back and forth, increasing in speed. Layeville had pounded futilely at the glass, screaming. The faces became blurred, were only tearing pink blobs before him.

On and on like this-for how long?

He hadn't minded it so much at first, that first nite. He couldn't sleep, but it was not uncomfortable. The lites of the city were comets with tails that pelted from rite to left like foaming fireworks. But as the nite wore on he felt a gnawing in his stomach, that grew worse. He got very sick and vomited. The next day he couldn't eat anything.

They never stopped the pendulum, not once. Instead of letting him eat quietly, they slid the food down the stem of the pendulum in a special tube, in little round parcels that plunked at his feet. The first time he attempted eating he was unsuccessful, it wouldn't stay down. In desperation he hammered against the cold glass with his fists until they bled, crying hoarsely, but he heard nothing but his own weak, fear-wracked words muffled in his ears.

After some time had elapsed he got so that he could eat, even sleep while travelling back and forth this way. They allowed him small glass loops on the floor and leather thongs with which he tied himself down at nite and slept a soundless slumber without sliding.

People came to look at him. He accustomed his eyes to the swift flite and followed their curiosity-etched faces, first close by in the middle, then far away to the right, middle again, and to the left.

He saw the faces gaping, speaking soundless words, laughing and pointing at the prisoner of time traveling forever nowhere. But after awhile the town people vanished and it was only tourists who came and read the sign that said: THIS IS THE PRISONER OF TIME-JOHN LAYEVILLE-WHO KILLED THIRTY OF THE WORLDS FINEST SCIENTISTS! The school children, on the electrical moving sidewalk stopped to stare in childish awe. THE PRISONER OF TIME!

Often he thot of that title. God, but it was ironic, that he should invent a time machine and have it converted into a clock, and that he, in its pendulum, should mete out the years-traveling *with* Time.

He couldn't remember how long it had been. The days and nites ran together in his memory. His unshaven checks had developed a short beard and then ceased growing. How long a time? How long?

Once a day they sent down a tube after he ate and vacuumed up the cell, disposing of any wastes. Once in a great while they sent him a book, but that was all.

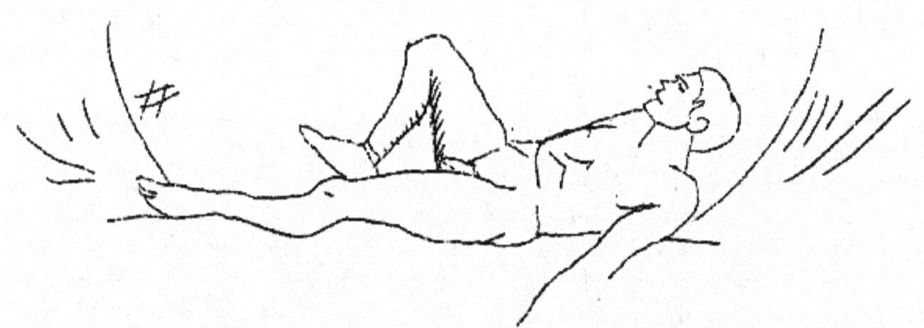

The robots took care of him now. Evidently the humans thot it a waste of time to bother over their prisoner. The robots brot the food, cleaned the pendulum cell, oiled the machinery, worked tirelessly from dawn until the sun crimsoned westward. At this rate it could keep on for centuries.

But one day as Layeville stared at the city and its people in the blur of ascent and descent, he perceived a swarming darkness that extended in the heavens. The city rocket ships that crossed the sky on pillars of scarlet flame darted helplessly, frightenedly for shelter. The people ran like water splashed on tiles, screaming soundlessly. Alien creatures fluttered down, great gelatinous masses of black that sucked out the life of all. They clustered thickly over everything, glistened momentarily upon the pendulum and its body above, over the whirling wheels and roaring bowels of the metal creature once a Time Machine. An hour later they dwindled away over the horizon and never came back. The city was dead.

Up and down, Layeville went on his journey to nowhere, in his prison, a strange smile etched on his lips. In a week or more, he knew, he would be the only man alive on earth.

Elation flamed within him. This was *his* victory! Where the other men had planned the pendulum as a prison it had been an asylum against annihilation now!

Day after day the robots still came, worked, unabated by the visitation of the black horde. They came every week, brot food, tinkered, checked, oiled, cleaned. Up and down, back and forth-THE PENDULUM!

...a thousand years must have passed before the sky again showed life over the dead Earth. A silvery bullet of space dropped from the clouds, steaming, and hovered over the dead city where now only a few solitary robots performed their tasks. In the gathering dusk the lites of the metropolis glimmered on. Other automatons appeared on the rampways like spiders on twisting webs, scurrying about, checking, oiling, working in their crisp mechanical manner.

And the creatures in the alien projectile found the time mechanism, the pendulum swinging up and down, back and forth, up and down. The robots still cared for it, oiled it, tinkering.

A thousand years this pendulum had swung. Made of glass the round disk at the bottom was, but now when food was lowered by the robots through the tube it lay untouched. Later, when the vacuum tube came down and cleaned out the cell it took that very food with it.

Back and forth-up and down.

The visitors saw something inside the pendulum. Pressed closely to the glass side of the cell was the face of a whitened skull —a skeleton visage that stared out over the city with empty sockets and an enigmatical smile wreathing its lipless teeth.

Back and forth-up and down.

The strangers from the void stopped the pendulum in its course, ceased its swinging and cracked open the glass cell, exposing the skeleton to view. And in the gleaming light of the stars the skull face continued its weird grinning as if it knew that it had conquered something. Had conquered time.

The Prisoner Of Time, Layeville, had indeed travelled along the centuries.

And the journey was at an end.

Is It True What They Say About Kuttner? Or The Man With The Weird Tale
by Guy Amory

The extremely interesting specimen to your right is not a head from a formaldehyde jar, though at times we have seen it, or him, pickled. It is I, Henry Kuttner, the laziest man who ever punched a typewriter and got paid for it. Like several other L.A. natives he is too busy living to do much worrying-and besides-what does it get him? (a check from Weird Tales) Henry has just sold them a 20,000 word yarn about Elak of Atlantis. At present he has finished a story headed for STARTLING, fifty thousand words or more, and been working with C. L. Moore on a new chiller.

Hank's first story for Astounding was a disappointment, but he fully made up for that by turning in a sockerooo to Unknown called *the misguided halo*, written after the fashion of his most highly cherished author THORNE SMITH. What the fans don't know is that this little tale had a different ending than the one used by Campbell. Kuttner's finis to the halo was hysterically funny, but John W. thought otherwise and tagged a new finish on it-spoiling it as far as this author is concerned.

Kuttner is 24 years old. He's been writing most of his life-learned how to type at the age of eight and hasn't left it alone since. Was born with a type-bar in his mouth. Lives in a quiet catacomb called Beverly Hills, the first cemetery I've ever seen with street lamps. At present, though I have broached the subject on numerous occasions, Hank steadfastly refuses to write for slick magazines. His best excuse being his laziness.

Hanks is quiet-speaking, sincere. But he has a sense of humor, the kind that hits you amidriff abruptly. He is the perfect dead-pan jokester. His digs many times being too subtle for your correspondent to catch until several moments have passed, Kuttner is always ready to rush in mildly and put the immature fans to route. It is only when you see the ghastly pictures that he takes out at his charnal cave that you realize his true sense of comedy. He and Hodgkins and Shroyer, the fiends, get together in outre garb, in horrifying pose, and bring forth films that would shake the mind of even such a horror as Robert Bloch.

Kuttner likes the way C. L. Moore writes (and who doesn't). He wishes he could write like her-but claims that when he tries imitating it comes out so much trash. If you've read any of his stories you realize that Hank is a master of the bingety-boom type of fiction-but with feeling! He puts more Incident in ten pages of Elak than any other author in WEIRD, and makes you feel it. He paints his picture with masterfully abrupt dabs, while Moore lays on her horror with the touch of a mosaic master, building up. Kuttner knocks you down and keeps you bouncing. Moore swirls you in cobwebs and totes you away into infinity. Combining their efforts in '37 for QUEST OF THE STARSTONE they turned out something to remember ... with Hank's flair for lightning pace and Moore's for description they went to town.

That's about all we can say about Hank, He doesn't like New York because it's too dirty, noisy and big. He dotes on Thorne Smith. Rite now he's trying to crash Argosy with a story-and in the future you can expect some big things from this quiet author.

Oh, yes, and is it true what they say about Kuttner?

No, he doesn't use dope to get the effect in his stories. He has a massive painting of Art Barnes on his desk and when he prepares to write he squints once and once only at that painting to get gruesome atmosphere. Then he starts typing!

Take a bow, Mr. Kuttner.

(Jus bend over a little more, Hank! A' K' BARNES)

WHUMP!

Ouch! (KUTTNER)

The End (of Kuttner)

Analysis

FROM J CHAPMAN MISKE: Pretty snappy cover on the 1st issue of fufa. At least I like it. Simple stuff looks best on mimeod covers. By the way, what, I'd like to know, is the sex of that Bokian creature? WHY MR. MISKE! WE THOT U ABHORED SEX! TSK! TSK! I'm for Technocracy. Personally I suspect Reynolds of being Kuttner NOPE....TRY AGAIN, JACK. Your poetry not so hot. U wandered a bit and were melodramatic.

DALE HART POSTS: Bok cover good. Yerke and Reynolds interesting. Forrie's story unique. Yur poem full of thot but it didn't scan very well. MAYBE IT'S BECUZ I'M MORE BRITISH THAN I AM *SCAN*-DIN-AVIAN. (BRAD) How about an increase in pages-this issue much too small. HOPE YU LIKE THIS BIGGER SIZE, DALE.

GERTRUDE HEMKIN MUMBLES: Cover startling, technocracy article sounds sensible, ron reynolds satire amusing and contains a few kernels of logic, at that. And where hav I red 4SJ's RECORD bee4?

(WE *Wonder*) HENRY HASSE TYPES: "Hans Bok steals 1st honors 4 his cover. Hope yu can get Hans to do all yur illustrations each month." YES; HENRY, WE'LL HAVE BOK ON THE COVER EVERY ISSUE FROM NOW ON EVEN THO HE'S BUSY IN NEW YORK WITH HIS PANTING-SINCE THE EDITORIAL FOR FUFA WAS STENCILED THE DECEMBER ISSUE OF WEIRD TALES HAS APPEARED ON THE STANDS ALL OVER AMERICA WITH ITS COVER DONE BY BOK. IT WAS FUTURIA FANTASIA'S PLEASENT DUTY, THIS SUMMER; TO BRING ABOUT THAT DEAL BETWEEN BOK AND WEIRD AND WE ARE JUSTLY PROUD OF HANS AND HIS SUCCESS. HERE'S HOPING HE HITS ASTOUNDING NEXT. HASSE CONTINUES: "Best written feature was yur poem, Brad. Next is Reynolds piece and the one by Ackerman." DUE TO LACK OF SPACE IN THIS ISSUE WE ARE CONDENSING THE ABOVE LETTERS. IN THE WINTER EDITION THERE WILL BE A BIGGER LETTER DEPARTMENT-THAT IS, IF YU WRITE IN. WE'RE ANXIOUS TO KNOW HOW YOU LIKED OUR SPECIAL *the pendulum*. UNTIL THEN, FU, FAREWELL!

Return From Death
by Antony Corvais

They were seated in his parked, car, miles from the city, when Robert told Ellen; "I'll always love you, darling, forever and ever. I just can't help myself, and I don't want to."

The girl nestled closer without reply.

"And if something should happen to one of us, the other would wait-because love like ours will never know death-it must go on-for eternity," he continued. "I know that I'll love you even when I'm dead, and if there are such things as spirits, I'll come back to you-somehow. Or would it frighten you?"

Ellen pouted: "Don't be so funereal! It makes me feel strangely inside. Of course nothing can separate us. It's a beautiful nite and we're wasting it on-oh, dear!" Her eyes had glanced at the small clock on the paneling. "It's late, Robert. You must hurry me home now or mother will be furious!"

Sighing, Robert started the car. As they roared toward town over the twisting roadway, suddenly the car swerved.

"Lookout, Bob! A man!" It was Ellen's high voice screaming.

The car skidded sickeningly on loose gravel, crashed thunderously through the railing bordering the highway, and richocheted, turning over and over, halting as wreckage. Robert was crushed under the metal bulk, losing consciousness.

Thrown clear, Ellen scrambled to the man, bent over him. Something more than pain filmed his eyes; he heard himself muttering: "I'll come back? —you wait —" in a failing whisper as illimitable darkness swept over him, accompanied by dreadful nausea. A point of light appeared in the void, expanding into a dazzling rectangle which split into thousands of lesser planes; these shaped a geometric pattern which whirled dizzily, humming, the drone rising in pitch with every sickening revolution, becoming incessant mechanical scream — —

"And this is death. This is past human endurance." With sudden omniscience he knew that he WAS dead and the meaning of the spinning pattern. The knowledge ebbed and carried with it all of his memories except for Ellen's face and her name.

The wheeling design parted like a curtain, and Robert observed beyond it a branching path spreading before him like a flattened tree. At the end of every fork was Ellen's face, wavering and blurred. He fixed his attention upon the nearest furcation, aspiring toward it desperately, and sensed himself hovering in space.

Shock, as of lightning coursing his veins, knotted him with agony. Involuntarily his eyes squeezed shut. Icy air tortured his lungs. As he raised his voice in weak protest, the pain ceased and he relaxed, spent. His eyes continued shut, as though the lids were gummed down. Failing in many attempts to open them, he quested food, found it, and consoled himself with it.

Occasionally plaintive voices babbled unintelligibly, arousing him. Always, if he listened, he heard a gentle murmur reply to the voices. And then everything was quiet. He felt very sleepy. Finally he dropped off into slumber, deep and restful.

Between periods of sleep, Robert struggled with his heavy eyelids. Memories might have associated his sightlessness with blindness-but he had none. There were only Ellen's face and her name which, when expecially desperate, he called again and again.

Gradually his vision became clear, and he stared in awe at a world of immensity which was peopled with Titans. The picture of Ellen in this gigantic place troubled him, for the colossal beings looked upon him as an animated toy. Often he was elevated to their reeking mouths, kissed, and dropped aside; if he were insistent upon attention, inquiring for Ellen, the giants beat him and thrust him from their presence.

Inert bare-surfaced looming things inclosed him, from some of which, when he approached them, he was kicked away. Incredibly huge portals barred egress to an outer world, from which seeped strange sharp odors. By calling his one word to the world beyond the doors, Robert endeavored to explain to the Titans that Ellen might possibly be outside. But they hushed him with amusement, sometimes with abuse.

There had been others prisoned here like himself while he had not seen, but they had vanished now, but this bothered him not in the least-his thoughts were of Ellen, and finally the giants lifted him and put him into a windowless room and clamped a fretted ceiling over it. The chamber rocked gently; he realized that it was being moved from one place to another. Leaping frantically he touched the ceiling's lattice, clung to it, struggling to force himself through its interstices. Unsuccessful, tiring, he fell back, crouched in a corner, weeping.

Motion of transit ended-the confining ceiling vanished. Robert scrambled over a wall, dropped to the ground of the outer world, whose heavy conflicting odors, dazzling lights and moving shadows alarmed him. Dim with distance was the withdrawing form of a giant, which he pursued, crying out his one word, "ELLEN!"

The giant vanished among weird wavering plants. Alone, Robert skulked nervously through tall rustling things, was terrified at times by an unexpected sound or motion. But the swaying things appeared unaware of him and he became self-confidant. Discovering a stretch of damp earth gemmed with puddles, he drank. His head cocked at a sound reminiscent of Ellen: her soothing voice.

A giantess had appeared over him. She was-ELLEN! At sight of her, Robert's pent memories burst free, overwhelming his consciousness with turbulent pageantry. He thrust up his arms; gently indulgent, the girl bent and drew him to her breast. She cuddled him, cooing to him. At the moment her monstrous size did not concern him.

"I've found you! I've found you!" he cried. "Oh, Ellen, if only you knew how lonely it has been —" He opened his glad heart to her in a stammering urgency, bliss in his eyes, tears in his voice. Breathless, he raised his face to the girl's; she hesitated. Then she kissed him and set him down at her feet. She strode away. Crying with hurt amazement, he followed. She shook her head. She kept walking swiftly. He could not keep up with her and he stopped forlornly as she disappeared behind an obstruction. He stared after her with unbelieving eyes. Tho mysteriously stunted, he had returned to her from death, and she had not accepted him. He stepped close to one of her prodigious footprints in the mud and surveyed it grimly. His eyes sought an impression of his own foot. And suddenly he cried in mingled grief and horror-for there in the mud was his footprint-small-strange-the footprint of a half-grown cat!

Conventional Notes or the Report on the S.F.L. Ball Game
by The Editor

score: 27 sprained ankles to 3 cracked knees.

Ross Rocklynne: Tall, freckled, red haired, pleasent looking, good-natured and humorous-that is Rocklynne-and, by the way, in real life he spells it Rock*lin*. Makes the ideal traveling companion. Continually clicking away with his candid camera. Is versed in many subjects-likes plots about gigantic ideas, such as THE MOTH, giant men, and THE MEN AND THE MIRROR with an amorphous reflector, while JUPITER TRAP gave us a giant siphon. Rocklynne, 26, looks 22 or younger. Favorite expression, when agreeing with anyone is, "That's right." Spending most of my time after the convention with Ross, painting the town a delicate pink, I found that he is now trying a bit of Weird writing which has been unsuccessful, and some Western concocting-ditto. Ross is quite different than his characters Deveral and Colbie. Somehow I had imagined a Rocklynne with a sharp gaunted face and bulging muscles —I found, instead, a good example of what mite be called typical college species number #569Z, a cross between science and wit, well mixed and jelled in an Empire State tall body. Lives in Cincinnatti. His characters, Colbie and Deveral, are two of the most consistent and popular guys in s.f. today, according to Campbell.

Charlie Hornig: The dark horse who says neigh to every manuscript I write for him. Dark-haired, dark-eyed, dark-skinned fiend who deals from the bottom of the manuscript pile over at *Science-fiction*. He has just learned to speak English during the past week and now he finds it much more fun picking out the manuscripts instead of leaping into a pile of them and bobbing up with one between his teeth. Makes lousy speeches. Is a human dynamo and expert guide to anyone in Manhattan. Makes money on the side selling shoestrings on the I.R.T. between the Bronx and Coney Island. Father was a toupee manufacturer which makes Charlie hair to a big-wig's fortune. Thanx, Charlie, for your presence in New York to guide me around. And I just LOVE Science Fiction! (paid adv.)

Impressions cawt short: John W. (werewolf) Campbell, a scientific theory in a potato sack suit with high rubber boots to match.

Julius Schwartz and Groucho Marx look-alikes.

Mort Weisinger, a plump smile.

A. Merritt, the man on the billboards with a mug of Milwaukee beer in his hand. Jovial, glasses, chubby. Not a bit mysterious.

Forrest J. Ackerman, dressed in future garb at convention, looking like a fugitive from a costume shop.

Willy Ley, a pair of thick-lensed glasses with an accent. Lowndes-moustache and gold tooth-double feature. Leslie Perry-Madame Butterfly with bangs.

Henry Kuttner, a voice from a pile of cigarettes. Morojo, short and sweet, commonly referred to as the VOICE OF MIDGE. Sykora, nervous breakdown with hair. Moskowitz, human fog-horn: following his opening speech New York gripped by earth tremors. Wollheim, Communist, born in a revolving door, believes in revolutions, get it? Or do you? Sykora, Moskowitz, Taurasi-three little pigs. Manly Wade Wellman-the human JELL-O! Kornbluth, a well-padded belch. Swisher, massive literary Babe Ruth, king of so-what! Robert J. Thompson, the leaning tower of Pisa wired for sound.

Futuria Fantasia III

Gorgono *and* Slith —
by Ray Bradbury

"Let us, by all means, be lucid," said Gorgono to Slith. Slith fluttered his reptile tongue and turned his morbid eyes to me. "Yes," he said, "let us, certainly be lucid, Bradbury. From now on use a contents page in Futuria Fantasia." And he spanked his tail slickly on my typewriter.

I don't mind Slith so much, he's only a little anachronistic reptile, a descendent of happier days in dinosaurial dawndom. I never feared Slith. But Gorgono!

Gorgono pierced me with his slanting green, clear eyes, heavy-lidded, extending one claw and attempting to keep it from shaking while his pointed ears stood up straight. A moment before he had been hunting fleas in the fertile hair that clothed his muscular limbs, but now he was serious; so very serious it frightened me.

And when the thunder-voiced, evil-eyed, shaggy haired and monstrous Gorgono reclined on the shelf over my head, saliva drooling with silent precision from his pendulous lips, and gave orders I hastened to obey them. Gorgono was the voice of the critics-the ogre of opinion, the harsh guttural commandment of style and fashion. And now Gorgono had grumbled, "Number your pages from now on, MISTER Bradbury or else YOUR number'll be up. Why, Gad, man, the last issue of Futuria Fantasia I didn't know if I was coming or going, the way you heiroglyphed the sheets. And I might add, you're going to use even margins from here on in."

"Okay, okay, okay," I said, slinking with flushed visage behind my stencils. "But from now on Futuria Fantasia will be ten cents straight an issue. Ten cents straight." "Agreed," snapped Gorgono, "if you are neater. But you must be new, neotiric, different." Then I flashed them the newly processed cover done by Bok. "Gods!" bellowed Gorgono. "That is stupendous! A fine beginning, mortal, a very fine beginning!" Slith agreed by pounding vigorously on the table with his scaly rump. "And wait until you read Monroe's yarn," I jubilantly exclaimed. "It's not science-fiction, but it's certainly a fine bit of story." "Yes," said Gorgono, "this issue looks much better. Glad to see you've added two new authors, Damon Knight and Joe Kelleam from Astounding. I'll have to remind the fans to send in their dimes for this issue and perhaps support you a little more than they have with letters. But we'll see about that." He got up, stretched, yawned, and vanished in a belching ball of flame. "Yes," said Slith, "we'll see!" And he too vanished with a sharp pop. All was quiet. I went back to my stencils and my opium.

THE EDITOR.

Heil!
by Lyle Monroe

"How dare you make such a suggestion!"

The state physician doggedly stuck by his position. "I would not make it, sire, it your life were not at stake. There is no other surgeon in the Fatherland who can transplant a pituitary gland but Doctor Lans."

"You will operate!"

The medico shook his head. "You would die, Leader. My skill is not adequate. And unless the operation takes place at once, you will *certainly* die."

The Leader stormed about the apartment. He seemed about to give way to one of the girlish bursts of anger that even the inner state clique feared so much. Surprisingly he capitulated.

"Bring him here!" he ordered.

DOCTOR LANS FACED THE LEADER with inherent dignity, a dignity and presence that three years of "protective custody" had been unable to shake. The pallor and gauntness of the concentration camp lay upon him, but his race was used to oppression. "I see," he said. "Yes, I see ... I can perform that operation. What are your terms?"

"Terms?" The Leader was aghast. "Terms, you filthy swine? You are being given a chance to redeem in part the sins of your race!"

The surgeon raised his brows. "Do you not think I *know* that you would not have sent for me had there been any other course available to you? Obviously, my services have become valuable."

"You'll do as you are told! You and your kind are lucky to be alive."

"Nevertheless I shall not operate without my fee."

"I said you were lucky to be alive —" The tone was an open threat.

Lans spread his hands. "Well —I am an old man...."

The Leader smiled. "True. But I am informed that you have a —a family...."

The surgeon moistened his lips. His Emma-they would hurt his Emma ...and his little Rose. But he must be brave, as Emma would have him be. He was playing for high stakes-for all of them. "They cannot be worse off dead," he answered firmly, "than they are now."

It was many hours before the Leader was convinced that Lans could not be budged. He should have known-the surgeon had learned fortitude at his mother's breast.

"What is your fee?"

"A passport for myself and my family."

"Good riddance."

"My personal fortune restored to me —"

"Very well."

" —to be paid in gold before I operate!"

The Leader started to object automatically, then checked himself quickly. Let the presumptuous fool think so! It could be corrected after the operation.

"And the operation to take place in a hospital on foreign soil."

"Preposterous."

"I must insist."

"You do not trust me?"

Lans stared straight back into his eyes without replying. The Leader struck him, hard, across the mouth. The surgeon made no effort to avoid the blow, but took it, with no change of expression.

"YOU ARE WILLING TO GO THROUGH WITH IT, SAMUEL?" The younger man looked at Doctor Lans without fear as he answered,

"Certainly, Doctor."

"I can not guarantee that you will recover. The Leader's pituitary gland is diseased; when I exchange it for your healthy one your younger one may not be able to stand up under it-that is the chance you take. Besides —a complete transplanting has never been done before."

"I know it-but I'm out of the concentration camp!"

"Yes. Yes, that is true. And if you do recover, you are free. And I will attend you myself, until you are well enough to travel."

Samuel smiled. "It will be a positive joy to be sick in a country where there are no concentration camps!"

"Very well, then. Let us commence."

They returned to the silent, nervous group at the other end of the room. Grimly the money was counted out, every penny that the famous surgeon had laid claim to before the Leader had decided that men of his religion had no need for money. Lans placed half of the gold in a money belt and strapped it around his waist. His wife concealed the other half somewhere about her ample person.

IT WAS AN hour and twenty minutes later that Lans put down the last instrument, nodded to the surgeons assisting him, and commenced to strip off operating gloves. He took one last look at his two patients before he left the room. They were anonymous under the sterile gowns and dressings. Had he not known, he could not have guessed dictator from oppressed. Come to think of it, with the exchange of those two tiny glands there was something of the dictator in his victim and something of the victim in the dictator.

DOCTOR LANS RETURNED TO THE hospital later in the day, after seeing his wife and daughter safely settled in a first class hotel. It was an extravagence, in view of his uncertain prospects as a refugee, but they had enjoyed no luxuries for years back *there* —he didn't consider it his home country-and it was justified this once.

He inquired at the office of the hospital for his second patient. The clerk looked puzzled. "But he is not here...."

"Not here?"

"Why, no. He was moved at the same time as His Excellency-back to your country."

Lans did not argue. The trick was obvious; it was too late to do anything for poor Samuel. He thanked his God that he had had the foresight to place himself and his family beyond the reach of such brutal injustice before operating. He thanked the clerk and left.

THE LEADER RECOVERED CONSCIOUSNESS AT LAST. His brain was confused-then he recalled the events before he had gone to sleep. The operation! —it was over! And he was alive! He had never admitted to anyone how terribly frightened he had been at the prospect. But he had lived-he had lived! He groped around for the bellcord, and failing to find it, gradually forced his eyes to focus on the room. What outrageous nonsense was this? This was no sort of a room for the Leader to convalesce in. He took in the dirty white-washed ceiling, and the bare wooden floor with distaste. And the bed! It was no more than a cot!

He shouted. Someone came in, a man wearing a uniform of a trooper in his favorite corps. He started to give him the tongue-lashing of his life, before having him arrested. But he was cut short.

"Cut out the racket, you unholy pig!"

At first he was too astounded to answer, then he shrieked, "Stand at attention when you address the Leader! Salute!"

The trooper looked dumbfounded at the sick man-so totally different in appearance from the Leader, then guffawed. He stepped to the cot, struck a pose with his right arm raised in salute. He carried a rubber truncheon in it. "Hail to our Leader!" he shouted, and brought his arm down smartly. The truncheon crashed into the sick man's cheek bone.

Another trooper came in to see what the noise was while the first was still laughing at his wittcism. "What's up, Jon? Say, you'd better not handle that monkey too rough-he's still carried on the hospital list." He glanced casually at the bloody face.

"Him? Didn't you know?" Jon pulled him to one side and whispered.

The second man's eyes widened; he grinned. "So? They don't want him to get well, eh? Well, I could use a little exercise this morning —"

"Let's get Fats," the other suggested. "He's always so very amusing with his ideas."

"Good idea." He stepped to the door and bellowed, "Hey, Fats!"

They didn't really start in on him until Fats was there to help.

THE END

The Phantoms
by — —Joseph E. Kellerman

All day they played among the purple flowers
That lay like frozen flames upon the lawn;
Or dreamed within the shadows of the towers
Whose turret tops were painted as the dawn.
Bright was the garden; peace went everywhere
There was no breath of movement nor any sound
Save butterflies that clove the heavy air,
Or when the bright fruit dropped slowly to the ground.
Then the flowers drooped, from sliver thorns that tore;
Too soon the sun had died in amber smoke,
And frightened now but silent as before
The phantoms watched the garden change its cloak.
Great sable moths flew out, and one by one
The towers melted with the fallen sun.

———————————————————————

This is a plug ♁ for the Voice of the Imagi-nation. price 10c from Box 6475 Met Sta Los Angeles Cal.

[*] The Art (Widner & otherwise) is a bit better.

Thoughts on the Worldstate
by Henry Kuttner

The hideous Mr. Kuttner returns with an equally hideous tale. We absolutely guarantee this story will induce nausea and slight regurgitation. Lead on, McKuttner!

I have, as usual, been brooding over the intricacies of modern civilization. It seems to me that life is a peculiarly futile business. This mood of mine may, perhaps, be attributed to my recent tragic encounter with a horse at the corner of 42nd and Broadway.

I shall not dwell upon that incident, save to mention briefly that horses should, at least, be careful of what they eat. One never knows the result of the most innocent action, and that, by imperceptible degrees, brings me to the subject of this article, PLAYING FAIR WITH FANS, or, FANTASTIC DECENCY.

It has been said (and very loudly, too) that fans fight a lot. Well, I do not care to refute that; I happen to know that a Californian fan, a Mr. Ackerman, is in the habit of knocking down visitors and kicking them in strategic places. The question naturally arises, does fantasy lead to sadism?

I am reminded of the remarkable case of Scarlett O'God, an ardent fan whose tininess led to her being occasionally called by the diminutive, or fanny. This may seem somewhat confusing at first glance. Let us, therefore, go hastily on to the next paragraph.

I should, perhaps, mention a mysterious white-bearded gentleman called Tarboth the damned, or Toby, since he played a significant role in the incident. It was he who listened, toying at his beard idly, while Scarlett feverishly upheld her position against the onslaughts of her foes. Just what caused the argument I cannot recall at the moment. Nor does it matter especially. I believe it had something to do with Scarlett's being locked out of the Sanctuary, or Washroom, by previous arrivals.

Mocked, scorned, and jeered at, Scarlett at first said nothing. Ultimately, however, she lost her temper and cursed her enemies roundly. "I would," she observed with feeling, "sell my soul to the devil in order to obtain vengeance!"

At this moment the white-bearded gentleman smiled unpleasantly and vanished. Simultaneously lightning struck the Sanctuary and demolished it, to the natural discomfiture of the occupants. Laughing in a triumphant manner, Scarlett departed.

But the seeds of doom were already sown within her soul. Not until she was soaked to the skin did she realize the ghastly and hideous truth. Then, looking up, she saw that above her hovered a small black cloud, from which rain was steadily descending. As she realized the terror of her position, black horror flooded the girl. SHE HAD BECOME ALLERGIC TO WEATHER!

Well, after that, of course, matters got steadily worse. She was driven from home, after blasting the bathtub and spoiling a valuable Angora kitten. (It was later made into a muff, but moths got into it. That, however, is another story, and not an especially good one.)

Poor Scarlett was excluded from all fan gatherings. Sun stroke and eclipse were her constant companions. She came with the deluge and was gone with the wind.

The girl was utterly friendless. She roamed wildly here and there, haggard, careworn and miserable, in a tattered gown made from the covers of AMAZING STORIES. At night people could hear her moaning under their windows, and they huddled closer to the fire, whispering, "Fetch aft the rum, Darby! Evil walks abroad tonight and I feel my soul shudder in me. No soda, thanks!"

Hopeless and forlorn, Scarlett stowed away on a schooner out for Hong Kong. But she was discovered, cursed for a Jonah, and set ashore on a cannibal isle in the South Seas.

It was a blessing in disguise. The natives mistook her for a goddess. They were used to bad weather, and did not attribute the altered climate to Scarlett.

So they garlanded her with leis and made her their queen.

And she rained happily ever after.

Would You?
by J. Harvey Haggard

Would you stroll with me, my loved one

'Neath the pale Venusian Moon,
Where its misty orb goes drifting,

Waning, darling, all too soon?
Would you gaze into the rainbow

Where the lunar moonbeams play,
Could it be you'd softly answer

"Yes, for all those things I pray?"
If it's so, my darling, kick me,

For I'd surely be a ninny,

Making love by Venus moonlight —

When-you see-there isn't any!

The Piper
by Ron Reynolds

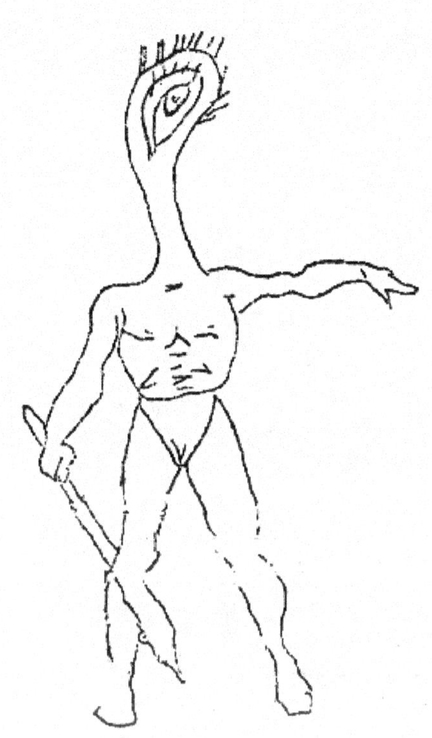

"LORD! HE'S THERE AGAIN! HE'S THERE! LOOK!" the old man croaked, jabbing a calloused finger at the burial hill. "Old Piper again! As crazy as a loon! Every year that way!"

The Martian boy at the feet of the old man stirred his thin reddish feet in the soil and affixed his large green eyes upon the burial hill where the Piper stood. "Why does he do that?" asked the boy.

"Ah?" The old man's leathery face rumpled into a maze of wrinkles. "He's crazy, that's what. Stands up there piping on his music from sunset until dawn."

The thin piping sounds squealed in the dusk, echoed back from the low hills, were lost in melancholy silence, fading. Then louder, higher, insanely, crying with shrill voice.

The Piper was a tall, gaunt man, face as pale and wan as Martian moons, eyes electrical purple, standing against the soft of the dusking heaven, holding his pipe to his lips, playing. The Piper —a silhouette —a symbol —a melody.

"Where did the Piper come from?" asked the Martian boy.

"From Venus." The old man took out his pipe and filled it. "Oh, some twenty years ago or more, on the projectile with the Terrestrians. I arrived on the same ship, coming from Earth, we shared a double seat together."

"What is his name?" Again the boyish, eager voice.

"I can't remember. I don't think I ever knew, really."

A vague rustling sound came into existence. The Piper continued playing, paying no heed to it. From the darkness, across the star-jewelled horizon, came mysterious shapes, creeping, creeping.

"Mars is a dying world," the old man said. "Nothing ever happens of much gravity. The Piper, I believe, is an exile."

The stars trembled like reflections in water, dancing with the music.

"An exile." The old man continued. "Something like a leper. They called him THE BRILLIANT. He was the epitome of all Venerian culture until the Earthmen came with their greedy incorporations and licentious harlots. The Earthlings outlawed him, sent him here to Mars to live out his days."

"Mars is a dying world," repeated the boy. "A dying world. How many Martians are there, sir?"

The old man chuckled. "I guess maybe you are the last pure Martian alive, boy. But there are millions of others."

"Where do they live? I have never seen them."

"You are young. You have much to see, much to learn."

"Where do they live?"

"Out there, beyond the mountains, beyond the dead sea bottoms, over the horizon and to the north, in the caves, far back in the subterrane."

"Why?"

"Why? Now that's hard to say. They were a brilliant race once upon a time. But something happened to them, hybrided them. They are unintelligent creatures now, cruel beasts."

"Does Earth own Mars?" The little boy's eyes were riveted upon the glowing planet overhead, the green planet.

"Yes, all of Mars. Earth has three cities here, each containing one thousand people. The closest city is a mile from here, down the road, a group of small metal bubble-like buildings. The men from Earth move about among the buildings like ants enclosed in their space suits. They are miners. With their huge machines they rip open the bowels of our planet and dig out our precious life-blood from the mineral arteries."

"Is that all?"

"That is all." The old man shook his head sadly. "No culture, no art, no purpose. Greedy, hopeless Earthlings."

"And the other two cities — —where are they?"

"One is up the same cobbled road five miles, the third is further still by some five hundred miles."

"I am glad I live here with you, alone." The boy's head nodded sleepily. "I do not like the men from Terra. They are despoilers."

"They have always been. But someday," said the old man, "they will meet their doom. They have blasphemed enough, have they. They cannot *own* planets as they have and expect nothing but greedy luxury for their sluggishly squat bodies. Someday — —!" His voice rose high, in tempo and pitch with the Piper's wild music.

Wild music, insane music, stirring music. Music to stir the savage into life. Music to effect man's destiny!

> "Wild-eyed Piper on the hill,
> Crying out your rigadoons,
> Bring the savages to kill
> 'Neath the waning Martian moons!"

"What is that?" asked the boy.

"A poem," said the old man. "A poem I have written in the last few days. I feel something is going to happen very soon. The Piper's song is growing more insistent every night. At first, twenty years ago, he played on only a few nights of every year, but now, for the last three years he has played until dawn every night of every autumn when the planet is dying."

"Bring the savages?" the boy sat up. "What savages?"

"There!"

Along the star-glimmered mountain tops a vast clustering herd of black, murmuring, advancing. The music screamed higher and higher.

> "Piper, pipe that song again!
> So he piped, I wept to hear."

"More of the poem?" asked the boy.

"Not my poem-but a poem from Earth some seventy years ago. I learned it in school."

"Music is strange." The little boy's eyes were scintillant with thought. "It warms me inside. This music makes me angry. Why?"

"Because it is music with a purpose."

"What purpose?"

"We shall know by dawn.

"Music is the language of all things-intelligent or not, savage or educated civilian. This Piper knows his music as a god knows his heaven. For twenty years he has composed his hymn of action and hate and finally, tonight perhaps, the finale will be reached. At first, many years ago, when he played, he received no answer from the subterrane, but the murmur of gibbering voices. Five years ago he lured the voices and the creatures from their caves to the mountain tops. Tonight, for the first time, the herd of black will spill over the trails toward our hovel, toward the road, toward the cities of man!"

Music screaming, higher, faster, insanely, sending shock after macabre shock thru night air, loosening the stars from their riveted stations. The Piper stretched high, six feet or more, upon his hillock, swaying back and forth, his thin shape attired in brown-cloth. The black mass on the mountain came down like amoebic tentacles, met and coalesced, muttering and mumbling. "Go inside and hide," said the old man. "You are young, you must live to propagate the new Mars. Tonight is the end of the old, tomorrow begins the new! It is death for the men of Earth!" Higher still and higher. "Death! They come to overrun the Earthlings, destroy their cities, take their projectiles. Then-in the ships of man-to Earth! Turnabout! Revolution and Revenge! A new civilization! When monsters usurp men and men's greediness crumbles at his demise!" Shriller, faster, higher, insanely tempoed. "The Piper-The Brilliant One-He who has waited for years for this night. Back to Venus to reinstall the glory of his civilization! The return of Art to humanity!"

"But they are savages, these unpure Martians," the boy cried.

"Men are savages. I am ashamed of being a man," the old man said, tremblingly. "Yes, these creatures are savages, but they will learn-these brutes-with music. Music in many forms — — music for peace, music for love-music for hate and music for death. The Piper and his brood will set up a new cosmos. He is immortal!" Now, hurrying, muttering up the road, the first cluster of black things reminiscent of men. A strange sharp odor in the air. The Piper, from his hillock, walking down the road, over the cobbles, to the city. "Piper, pipe that song again!" cried the old man. "Go and kill and live again! Bring us love and art again! Piper, pipe the song! I weep!" Then: "Hide, child, hide quickly! Before they come! Hurry!" And the child, crying, hurried to the small house and hid himself thru the night.

Swirling, jumping, running, leaping, gamboling, crying-the new humanity surged to man's cities, his rockets, his mines. The Piper's song! Stars shuddered. Winds stilled. Nightbirds sang no songs. Echoes murmured only the voices of the ones who advanced, bringing new understanding. The old man, caught in the whirlpool of ebon, was swept down, screaming. Then up the road, by the awful thousands, vomiting out of hills, sprawling from caves, curling, huge fingers of beasts, around and about and down to the Man Cities. Sighing, leaping up, voices and destruction!

Rockets across the sky!

Guns. Death.

And finally, in the pale advancement of dawn, the memory, the echoing of the old man's voice. And the little boy arose to start afresh a new world with a new mate.

Echoing, the old man's voice:

"Piper, pipe that song again! So he piped, I wept to hear!"

A new day dawned.

The End

The Itching Hour
by Damon Knight

Mind you, I don't believe the story, myself. It was obvious, from the start, that the old man was mad. Besides, I was stinko at the time, and I may not have got some of the details right. But in its essentials, the story still sticks in my mind....I can see the old man now, with a pair of my best socks around his neck, moaning and wheezing and spitting on the floor, and in between times telling his strange, strange story. Of course, the whole thing was fantastic; the old loon had probably escaped from some nut factory....and yet....No, no, the old man was booby. And yet....And yet....

The night it happened I was sitting in my study in my white silk Russian lounging robe, smoking a narghile or Indian water-pipe and throwing darts at a signed photograph of Sally Rand. I'd just pinked her neatly in the gluteus maximus, when I was startled by a crash of glass, and turned around to see an aged man tottering carefully thru the remains of my French windows.

At once the chill of horror griped me. Oops, I mean *gripped*!! Unable to move, I stared speechlessly as the old man went directly to my chest of drawers and fumbled within, the overhead light throwing his face into sombre shadow.

Blowing his nose on one of my dress shirts he grumbled to himself about the starch and selected a pair of lamb's wool socks and tied them around his neck. This done, he hobbled over to a chair facing mine, sat down, pulled his tattered undershirt, which for some reason he was wearing as a shawl, more closely around his thin shoulders, stared reproachfully at me, shivering at the icy blast that came in thru the shattered windows. "There's a draft in here, and you know what you can do about it," he complained.

"Yes, there is," I managed to get out.

He nodded, satisfied. "I thought there was," he said. Then, dragging his chair closer, he leaned over and, grasping me firmly by the lapels, said pleasantly, "Ipswitch on the amscray, don't you think?"

Half stifled with terror, I gasped, "Uh, yes." At once his manner was transformed. Drawing himself up indignantly he sneered "That's a lie! That's what they all say, the sniveling hypocrites! They know it's a lie!"

Then he drew nearer once again. "But," he said, "I'm going to tell you my story anyway. You have a kind face. And I —I just don't have any at all." He raised the rim of his hat and I saw it was true! He had no face! Gibbering, I tried to get away, to flee or scram, but it was too late. Taking a firmer grip on my lapels, and standing heavily on my foot, the old man began his story.

"You may not believe it (he began) but I, too, was once a carefree young fan like yourself. From morning til night I thot of nothing but eating, sleeping, sex, and my fan-mag, PUKE. In the evening I would stay up til morning, splashing happily in my hecto inks, and turning out pages and pages of material like mad. And at last I'd go to bed, tired but happy, knowing I had done my duty as an honest fan.

"And then, one day, it happened. By some unfortunate chance, I got a little double-strength purple hectograph ink on my face. Noticing it in the mirror the next morning, as I was trying to decide whether to shave this week or not, I took a washcloth and tried to rub off the stain. Alas, poor fool that I was, I recked not of the consequences!

"With hard rubbing, I managed to get some of the ink off, but when I went on rubbing, to remove the rest, the ink I had rubbed off was transferred back to my face. And so it went, the adament ink going from washrag to face and from face back to washrag.

"The ink, as I have said, was double-strength purple undiluted, and suffered nothing in the process. But something had to give way. The washrag, by an unhappy coincidence, was a brand-new one, and my face was some years old. Only one thing could have happened. It did."

Thus, shedding a tear on the carpet, the old stranger ended his weird tale. Getting slowly to his feet, he drew his hat down over his eyes once more, tied his socks around his neck more tightly, and shuffled off toward the shattered windows. At the sill, he turned, faced the room, and made one last parting shot, ere he vanished in the gloom. *"Dogs have fleas!"* he screamed.

But sometimes I wonder.

I've Never Seen
by Hannes Bok

I've never seen a Flirtenflog.
I've heard that it's a Martian dog.
But science-fiction has romanced
That the Martian race is much advanced;
So thus my reasoning should be,

Has a Flirtenflog ever seen ME?????

Ninevah
by J. E. Kelleam

They say the bittern and the cormorant
Have nested in the upper lintels there.
The wind builds flowers of dust upon the air,
Lifting and falling, slow and hesitant.
Within the crumbling temples beasts have laired;
Eyeless the windows, broken the terraces;
No laughter breaks the silence. The palaces
Are weathered and the cedar work is bared.

If this be glory's wage, then let me trust
The fragile things that are not built of might,
The lovely things that leave no trace when gone:
The rose that swiftly turns into the dust,
Beauty that blazed a moment — —Or a night
Of golden stars forgotten with the dawn.

Futuria Fantasia IV

The Voice of Scariliop
by H. V. B.

Four pillars, arising out of the stone like strange growing things of demoniac shape-these Redforth saw and comprehended, knowing full well that Tarath had always abounded in monstrosities. "But what," he asked himself, "will knowing of such as this, be of use to me, as I search for Ghiltharmie?" For he had at last come to realise, to admit even to himself, that he was a lost thing. The Yulphog had taken his soul. They had exiled him to this lost land of dread. But they'd hinted of escape, if he could find it. "Si Yamlon," he had told him, pointing to a writhing belt of suns, lifting and lowering at the horizon like the yellow crest of a flaming wave. And he had nodded his head. They had vanished, disintegrating, it seemed. He didn't then know that they were related to Topper's friends and the jeep in one thing: that their Typonisif and Tregoifer was applicable to the atmosphere.

The four pillars were bending from their own weight. Strange colors-like an idiot's conception of a spectrum, spectrally rippled like irid waves across the columns. Like music in color. Assailed by their complex harmonies, Redforth could only stand speechless, hands thrust defensively forward. IT WAS THEN THAT HE SAW EIRY.

The pillars split. From each of then drifted a whiff of steam. They united into a wavering cloud which shimmered an instant in mid-air, then settled to the ground. And as it touched the metallic grass blades which stretched on and on like the upraised swords of a midget army, the vapor-cloud condensed into a woman's body. EIRY. Queen of Scariliop!

He recognized her at once, tho he had only read of her. She was not human. Her body was like a snake's, and she had bat wings. From a cluster of writhing worm-tentacles leered her face, like a mask in the heart of a seething flower. It was oval, and the scarlet mouth was like a velvet cushion-disproportionate-waiting for some priceless burden. Her nose was negligible, but her lone eye was vast and blue; like a doorway opening upon a sky too blue to belong to our world. Like blue incarnate: and blue is the color of MYSTERY.

She opened her mouth, and her tongue unrolled, uncoiled toward Redforth. Three feet long, the tongue was filamental, like a strand of red cobweb, tipped by a touch of fluff like a dandelion's seed. This member wandered lightly over Redforth's cheek, and for the first time EIRY spoke: "It comes to me that here is the man for whom we have been seeking, Yasgorphitove." Her voice was soft as clouds. Redforth in vain peered to behold her companion. "Now shall we enlighten him as to the ways of escape? In return for a favor, of course."

The air about her, for a fleeting instant, had turned blue. Then she nodded. She leaned forward, to whisper, but suddenly there was a crackling. "The rock!" she cried. "The rock! I must return before it is too late and I too am trapped!" She writhed, became coiling wreathes of smoke, and the smoke flowed back to the rocks, hovered over it. The four pillars quivered and joined into one and then, in a twinkling, had crumbled to powder.

But there was an uncanny blueness in the air about Redforth. And that night he had a dreadful dream.

For he had become-Yrthicaol! And EIRY had been merely-THE BAIT!

Aw G'Wan!
by Henry Hasse

THERE! If "Foo E. Onya", in the last issue, could use a pseudonym so can I. I read his article, I'M THROUGH, with varying degrees of interest. If an answer were really necessary, it could be found more appropriately in the two words of my title above, than in any words that might follow. And that brings up my first point in my rebuttal—

Why is it that people, including the lowly science-fiction fan, (to paraphrase Mr. Onya) always feel it necessary to hide behind a pseudonym when they have something to say which they think will displease someone? I've seen this happen so many times! And, coincidently, why SHOULD Mr. Onya take such pains to be unpleasent in print? Why should he feel it necessary to make one final, grand broadcast to the effect that he will no longer read paltry science-fiction? Does he think that any real lover of sci-fic gives a damn whether there is one less reader, especially a reader who crawls behind such a silly pseudonym as "Onya"? I've seen other broadcasts such as Mr. Onya's, and they always puzzled me. It surely can be nothing else but the egotistical urge.

But I'm convinced that Onya isn't half so bitter really against sci-fiction as he tries to pretend. He's not really through. Because anyone really bitter against and through with sci-fic would simply stop reading it, not start deriding it! And I doubt if any person, once a fan, has ever completely broken away from sci-fic, THEY ALWAYS COME BACK.

And right here I'd like to say that a good deal of my doubt as to Onya's sincerity is because I'm fairly certain of the fellow's real identity. The general tone of his article, and several clues he divulged, convince me I'm right. And if I AM right, I can assure you, Brad, and any other readers who nay have been picqued at Onya's tone, that he shouldn't be taken seriously, and the less attention paid to his rantings, the better. I'm sure Onya would feel flattered if he thot someone took his article so seriously as to answer it. Yet here I am answering it, and damned if I know why, except that I think I took some of Mr. Onya's phrasing personally, almost. I don't think he should have gone to the extent of calling names and using words such as "moronic", "arrogant", etc.

Aside from this his piece seemed to me a conglomeration of contradictions, inconsistencies, praises here, derisions there, pats on the back, exaggerations, sneers and scorn, and, oh yes, a book review. Yes, I liked and appreciated and mostly agreed with Onya's comments on BRAVE NEW WORLD. It's a book which I'm sure sure many of the *moronic* sci-fic fans appreciated as well as Mr, Onya. But here's where Mr. Onya's and my tastes differ slightly, for I *also* liked PLANET OF THE KNOB HEADS in the Dec. issue of SCIENCE FICTION, whereas Mr. Onya probably wouldn't deign to read it because it's in one of the pulp mags. that he so deplores; thereby Mr. Onya would be missing a really entertaining and meaningful piece of writing, but that's all right, since Mr. Onya's own words said: "There is so much else of importance that has been written—".

You know, somehow I cannot bring myself to be as vitriolic against Mr. Onya as he was against sfn at moments. He tried hard to work up a case against sfn, poor fellow, and became (to me at least) amusing instead of convincing. Do you know what I saw? I saw a person who is temporarily *satiated*, as he said, with sfn,—but more than that, a person who is merely trying to persuade *himself*, more than other people, that sfn is as bad as he painted it! Naturally every fan has his likes and dislikes of the various stories, authors and magazines. Some have more *dislikes* than likes. I think even I do. But it must be admitted that every once in a while, usually unexpectedly, there pops up a story which is a delectable gem and a masterpiece, either of ingenuity or writing or both. Then one is exultant, and one continues reading sfn, even some trite and bad sfn, knowing that regularly he will encounter one of the gems which he wouldn't have missed reading for the world! Meanwhile we have with us Clark Ashton Smith, C. L.

Moore, Stanton Coblentz (delightful sometimes, not always), A. Merritt, and an occasional few others, whose work I doubt if even Mr. Onya could glibly pronounce as ordinary pulp. And we did have Lovecraft, Weinbaum, Howard, and others of whom the same thing can be said.

Naturally, too, a lot of criticism can be directed against sfn and sfn readers. A lot of criticism can be directed against *everything*, and usually is, by certain people who take an unholy delight in it. I myself have sometimes snorted in wrath at the gross egotism and, yes, stupidity and childishness, of certain fans. I would have taken great delight in kicking their blooming teeth down their bloody well bally throats. But did I do this? Did I succumb to this desire? No, I did not. I never got close enough. A more important reason is that I had the patience to realize this type of fan is a minority (*not* a majority, Mr. Onya, by any means!). But what I did *not* do was write bitter articles about it.

Here is only one of Mr. Onya's inconsistencies: he makes such statements as "fans are arrogant, blind, critically moronic", etc. —and "editors and writers as well cannot see anything beyond their own perverted models." In virtually the next breath he admires P. Schuyler Miller's intellectuality. Yet P. Schuyler Miller continues to write sfn, reads it, and is one of the active fans.

Furthermore, I disagree outright and violently with Onya's statement, "When literature becomes possessed of *ideas as such*, it is no longer literature." And I'd like to challenge Onya to a further debate on this, if he *dares*. Also his statement about Wells' early stories. It so happens (what a coincidence!) that I also read Wells' EXPERIMENT IN AUTOBIOGRAPHY-and yes, while Wells did admit his early sfn stories were a preparation for his later and more serious writing, he did *not* disclaim them as not being literature of their own type. The trouble with Mr. Onya, I'm afraid, is that he has (deliberately?) lost sight of the fact that there is literature *and* literature. Instead, he wants everything to conform precisely to his own rather peculiar conception of literature. I'll make a statement right here that will undoubtedly shock Mr. Onya: I'll go so far as to say that pulp fiction, even the pulpiest of pulp fiction, is really and truly LITERATURE, insofar as it has its own special niche, its own certain purpose for being. There, I've said it! I'll admit, Mr. Onya, that it took a little courage to say it. But I ask all who read this, isn't it true when you come to think of it?

I have not dealt with Onya's article nearly to the extent that I might, but I don't think it's really necessary, mainly because, as I said, I have a very strong idea who Foo E. Onya is. I wish I could hazard my suspicion right here, but I'm so sure I'm right, and both the editor and Onya seem so determined to keep it secret, that I cannot be otherwise than silent. I will merely conclude by reiterating my doubt that you, "Foo E. Onya", are really disclaiming sfn. At least I hope you will continue both reading and writing it. But I swear, if I ever hear of you doing so, I shall feel sorely tempted to broadcast what a hypocrite you were with that article!

The Fight of the Good Ship Clarissa
by One Who Should Know Better

The space rocket Clarissa was nine days out from Venus. The members of the crew were also out for nine days. They were hunters, fearless expeditionists who bagged game in Venusian jungles. At the start of our story they are busy bagging their pants, not to forget their eyes. A sort of lull has fallen over the ship (Note: a lull is a time warp that frequently attacks rockets and seduces its members into a siesta). It was during this lull that Anthony Quelch sat sprawled at his typewriter looking as baggy as a bag of unripe grapefruit. ANTHONY QUELCH, the Cosmic Clamor Boy, with a face like turned linoleum on the third term, busy writing a book: "Fascism is Communism with a shave" for which he would receive 367 rubles, 10 pazinkas and incarceration in a cinema showing Gone With The Wind.

The boys upstairs were throwing a party in the control room. They had been throwing the same party so long the party looked like a worn out first edition of a trapeze artist. There is doubt in our mind as to whether they were trying to break the party up or just do the morning mopping and break the lease simultaneously. Arms, legs and heads littered the deck. The boys, it seems, threw a party at the drop of a chin. Sort of a space cataclysm with rules and little regulation-kind of an atomic convulsion in the front parlor. The neighbors never complained. The neighbors were 450 million miles away. And the boys were tighter than a catsup bottle at lunch-time. The last time the captain had looked up the hatch and called to his kiddies in a gentle voice, "HELL!" the kiddies had thrown snowballs at him. The captain had vanished. Clever way they make these space bombs nowadays. A few minutes previous the boys had been tearing up old Amazings and throwing them at one another, but now they contented themselves with tearing up just the editors. Palmer was torn in half and he sat in a corner arguing with himself about rejecting a story for an hour before someone put him through an orange juice machine killing him. (Orange juice sorry, now?)

And then they landed on Venus. How in heck they got back there so quick is a wonder of science, but there they were. "Come on, girls!" cried Quelch, "put on your shin guards, get out there and dig ditches for good old W.P.A. and the Rover Boys Academy, earth branch 27!"

Out into the staggering rain they dashed. Five minutes later they came back in, gasping, reeling. They had forgotten their corsets! The Venusians closed in like a million land-lords. "Charge, men!" cried Quelch, running the other way. And then-BATTLE! "What a fight; folks," cried Quelch. "Twenty thousand earth men against two Venusians! We're outnumbered, but we'll fight!" BLOOSH! "Correction-ten thousand men fighting!" KERBLOM! "One hundred men from earth left!" BOOM! "This is the last man speaking, folks! What a fight. I ain't had so much fun since-Help, someone just clipped my corset strings!" BWOM! "Someone just clipped me!"

The field was silent. The ship lay gleaming in the pink light of dawn that was just blooming over the mountains like a pale flower. The two Venusians stood weeping over the bodies of the Earthlings like onion peelers or two women in a bargain basement. One Venusian looked at the other Venusian, and in a high-pitched, hoarse, sad voice said: "Aye, aye, aye-THIS-HIT SHOODEN HEPPEN TO A DOG-NOT A DOIDY LEEDLE DOG!" And dawn came peacefully, like beer barrels, rolling.

The Intruder
by Emil Petaja

It was in San Francisco, on the walk above the sand and surf that pounded like the heart of the earth. There was wind, the sky and sea blended in a grey mist.

I was sitting on a stone bench watching a faint hint of distant smoke, wondering what ship it was and from what far port.

Mine was a pleasent wind-loneliness. So when he came, wrapped in his great overcoat and muffler, hat pulled down, and sat on my bench I was about to rise and leave him. There were other benches, and I was not in the mood for idle gossip about Hitler and taxes.

"Don't go. Please." His plea was authentic.

"I must get back to my shop," I said.

"Surely you can spare a moment." I could not even to begin to place the accent in his voice. Low as a whisper, tense. His deep-set eyes held me ... his face was pale and had a serenity born of suffering. A placcid face, not given to emotional betrayels, yet mystical. I sat down again. Here was someone bewilderingly strange. Someone I wouldn't soon forget. He moved a hand toward me, as tho to hold me from going, and I saw with mild curiosity that he wore heavy gloves, like mittens.

"I am not well. I ... I must not be out in the damp air," I said. "But today I just had to go out and walk. I had to."

"I can understand." I warmed to the wave of aloneness that lay in his words. "I too have been ill. I know you, Otis Marlin. I have visited your shop off Market Street. You are not rich, but the feel of the covers on a fine book between your hands suffices. Am I right?"

I nodded, "But how...."

"You have tried writing, but have had no success. Alone in the world, your loneliness has much a family man, harassed might envy."

"That's true," I admitted, wondering if he could be a seer, a fake mystic bent on arousing in me an interest in spiritism favorable to his pocket-book. His next words were a little amused, but he didn't smile.

"No, I'm not a psychic-in the ordinary sense, I've visited your shop. I was there only yesterday," he said. And I remembered him. In returning from my lunch I had met him coming out of my humble place of business. One glimpse into those brooding eyes was not a thing to soon forget, and I recalled pausing to watch his stiff-legged progress down the street and around the corner.

There was now a pause, while I watched leaves scuttling along the oiled walk in the growling wind. Then a sound like a sigh came from my companion. It seemed to me that the wind and the sea spoke loudly of a sudden, as tho approaching some dire climax. The sea wind chilled me as it had not before, I wanted to leave.

"Dare I tell you? DARE I!" His white face turned upward. It was as though he questioned some spirit in the winds.

I was silent; curious, yet fearful of what it might be he might not be allowed to tell me. The winds were portentously still.

"Were you ever told, as a child, that you must not attempt to count the stars in the sky at night-that if you did you might *lose your mind?*"

"Why, yes. I believe I've heard that old superstition. Very reasonable, I believe; based on the assumption that the task would be too great for one brain. I...."

"I suppose it never occurred to you," he interrupted, "that this superstition might hold even more truth than that, truth as malignant as it is vast. Perhaps the cosmos hold secrets beyond comprehension of man; and what is your assurance that these secrets are beneficent and kind? Is nature rather not terrible, than kind? In the stars are patterns-designs which if read, might lure the intrepid miserable one who reads them out of earth and beyond ...beyond, to immeasurable evil....Do you understand what I am saying?" His voice quivered metallically, was vibrant with emotion.

I tried to smile, but managed only a sickly grin. "I understand you, sir, but I am not in the habit of accepting nebulous theories such as that without any shred of evidence."

"There is, sad to say, only too much evidence. But do you believe that men have *lost their minds* from incessant study of the stars?"

"Perhaps some have, I don't know," I returned. "But in the South of this state in one of the country's leading observatories, I have a friend who is famous as an astronomer. He is as sane as you or I. If not saner." I tacked the last sentence on with significant emphasis.

The fellow was muttering something into his muffler, and I fancied I caught the words "danger ..." and "fools ..." We were silent again. Low dark clouds fled over the roaring sea and the gloom intensified.

Presently, in his clipt speech, the stranger said, "Do you believe that life exists on other planets, other stars? Have you ever wondered what kind of life might inhabit the other stars in this solar system, and those beyond it?" His eyes were near mine as he spoke, and they bewitched me. There was something in them, something intangible and awful. I sensed that he was questioning me idly, as an outlander might be questioned about things with which the asker is familiar, as I might ask a New Yorker, "What do you think of the Golden Gate Bridge?"

"I wouldn't attempt to guess, to describe, for instance, a Martian man," I said. "Yet I read with interest various guesses by writers of fiction." I was striving to maintain a mood of lightness and ease, but inwardly I felt a bitter cold, as one on the rim of a nightmare. I suddenly realized, with childish fear, that night was falling.

"Writers of fiction! And what if they were to *guess too well*? What then? Is it safe for them to have full rein over their imaginations? Like the star-gazers...." I said nothing, but smiled.

"Perhaps, man, there have been those whose minds were acute beyond most earthly minds-those who have guessed too closely to truth. Perhaps *those who are Beyond* are not yet ready to make themselves known to Earthlings? And maybe THEY, are annoyed with the puny publicity they receive from imaginative writers....Ask yourself, *what is imagination*? Are earth-minds capable of conceiving that which is not and has never been; or is this imagination merely a deeper insight into worlds you know not of, worlds glimpsed dimly in the throes of dream? And whence come these dreams? Tell me, have you ever awakened from a dream with the sinister feeling that all was not well inside your mind? —that while you, the real you, were away in Limbo —*someone* —some*thing* was probing in your mind, invading it and reading it. Might not THEY leave behind them in departure shadowy trailings of *their* own minds?"

Now I was indeed speechless. For a strange nothing had started my neck-hairs to prickling. Authors who might have guessed too well....Two, no three, writers whose stories had hinted at inconceivable yet inevitable dooms; writers I had known; had recently died, by accident.

"What of old legends? Of the serpent who shall one day devour the sun. That legend dates back to Mu and Atlantis. Who, man, was and is Satan? Christ? And Jehovah? benevolent and all-saving, were but a monstrous jest fostered by THEY to keep man blindly content, and keep him divided among himself so that he strove not to unravel the stars?"

"Man, in my foolish youth I studied by candleflame secrets that would scorch your very soul. Of women who with their own bare hands have strangled the children they bore so that the world might not know....Disease and sickness at which physicians throw up their hands in helpless bafflement. When strong men tear at their limbs and heads and agony-seeking to drive forth alien forces that have netted themselves into their bodies. I need scarcely recount them all, each with its own abominable significance. It is THEM. Who are eternal and nameless, who send their scouts down to test earth-man. Don't you realize that they have watched man creep out of primal slimes, take limbs and shamble, and finally walk? And that they are waiting, biding their time...." I shivered with a fear beyond name. I tried to laugh and could not. Then, bold with stark horror, I shouted quite loudly: "How do you know this? Are you one of THEM?" He shook his head violently. "No, no!" I made as to go, feeling an aching horror within me.

"Stay only a moment more, man. I will have pity on you and will not tell you all. I will not describe *them*. And I will not assay that which, when upon first seeing you here by the sea, *I first intended....*" I listened. Not daring to look at him; as in the grip of daemonaic dream. My fingers clutched at the edges of the bench so tightly that I have been unable to write with them until now. He concluded thus:

"So you see that I am everywhere a worldless alien. Sometimes this secret is too great for one mind to contain, and I must talk. I must feel the presence of someone human near me, else I shall attempt to commit suicide and again fail. It is without end-my horror. Have pity on me, man of earth, as I have had pity on you."

It was then that I gripped him by the shoulders and looked with pleading desperation into his staring eyes. "Why have you told me? What —" My voice broke. My hands fell to my sides. I shuddered.

He understood. Shrieked one word: "PITY!" into my insensible ear, and was gone.

That was 3 nites ago and each nite since has been hell. I cannot remember how long it was after the STRANGER left that I found myself able to move, to rise, hobble home, suddenly ancient with knowledge. And I cannot-WILL NOT-reveal to you all that I heard.

I thot myself insane, but after an examination, a physician pronounced me that I had been strained mentally. I am competent. But I wonder if he is wrong.

I view the silken stars tonight with loathing. HE sought to master their inscrutable secret meaning, and succeeded. He imagined, he dreamed; and he fed his sleep with potions, so that he might learn where his mind might be during sleep, and himself probe into the mind that wandered from space into his resting body-shell. I am no scientist, no bio-chemist, so I learned little of his methods. Only that he did succeed in removing his mind from Earth, and soaring to some remote world over and beyond this universe-where THEY dwell. And THEY knew him to be a mind of Earth, he told me. He but hinted of the evil he beheld, so potent with dread that it shattered his mind. And THEY cured him, and sent him back to earth...."They are waiting!" he shrieked, in his grating skeleton of a voice. "They are contemptuous of man and his feeble colonies. But they fear that some day, like an overgrown idiot child, he may do them harm. But before this time-when Man has progressed into a ripeness-THEY will descend! Then they will come in hordes to exploit the world as THEY did before!"

Of his return, and his assuming the role of a man, the Alien spoke evasively. It was to be assurred that this talk of his was not some repulsive caprice; to know that all of it was true, that I gripped him and beheld him. To my everlasting horror, I must know. Little in itself, what I saw, but sufficient to cause me to sink down on the stone bench in a convulsive huddle of fear. Never again in life can I tear this clutching terror from my soul. Only this: That when I looked into his staring eyes in the dimness of murky twilight, and before he understood and quickly avaunted, I glimpsed with astoundment and repugnance that between the muffling of his coat and black scarf *the INTRUDER wore a meticulously painted metal mask-to hide what I must not see....*

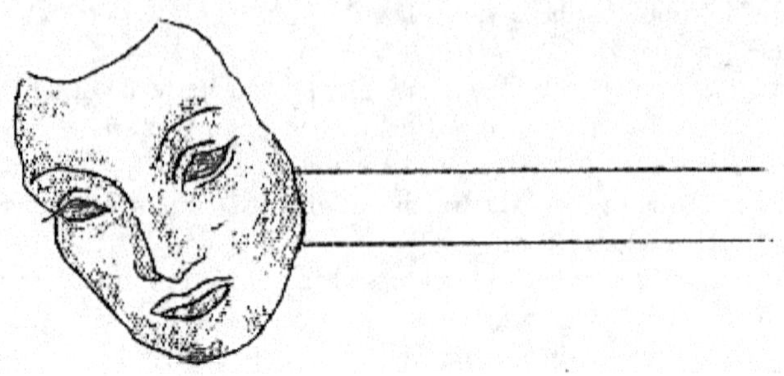

Asphodel:
by E. T. Pine

Down where skies are always dark,
Where is ever heard the bark
Of monstrous ebon hounds of hell,
In a dreadful fearsome knell,
Never fading, ever bright,
With a weird and spectral light,
Blooms a flower of ancient days,
Shining in a crimson maze;
When the black bat shrilly screams
Asphodel, you haunt my dreams —

From the lands of distant death
Steals the perfume of your breath:

Some night soon the wind will blow
Saffron seeds to fall and grow
By my casement window, where,
Sleeps my loved one, still and fair;
Then, the night you are to bloom
I shall creep from out my room,
From your blossom by the wall
Shall I hear her dear voice call:
Mournfully the wind will cry,
And shadows cover all the sky —
My lips will touch the loved dead

When where you nod I lay my head....

Marmok
by Emil Pataja

Sleep that doth harbour a dream of dread,
Whence come the fingers that beckoned and led
My dream-stung soul from my canopied bed —
Whither dost take me, ere I am dead?
Beyond the skull-grinning mid-March moon
Over the phosphorous-lit lagoon
Out past the darkest pits of the night,
Fast thru the stars in this evil flight;
Lead thee me out past the rim of space,
Show me that ravenous, pain-black face,
Marmok, whose myrmidons ever are questing
For souls who wander at nite, unresting.
Then shall I know an ultimate bliss
Tasting the fury of that cosmic kiss,
Whilst my earth-cloak lies limply on the floor
To waken and gibber forevermore.

What is the dim monstrosity that shimmers across the stars, what hand is that to cradle planets, earth and mars. What misshapen gargantuan of nebulous formed flesh, hurls out its flood of darkness, the systems to enmesh. What is it walks across the universes chanting cosmic choruses with endless verses-what thing unutterable has visited our Earth long years ago, and now, tonite, returns, in the shadows lurking glow. What ancient fear is with me, cold and terrible? Is that the shape of man upon the constellations, blotting out the light-or something gasping in hideous delight, plucking at the planets in insanity, at play, causing suns to boil like cauldrons, meteors to sing upon their way with mournful voices, lost ghosts upon lonely trails-wailing-wailing. Is tonight our rendezvous with the Cosmos Thing, the Colossus bigger than Andromeda that sits upon the throne of space-or are these fantasies upon my aged eyes?

Hades

Upon the shores of molten seas stand men, stand men alone,
And down below, in the molten flow, in the waves that cry and moan
Are women bare with flaming hair, whose passions have no surcease.
And in the air, midst the scarlet glare, are more who will never know Peace.

The Best Ways To Get Around

I don't mean socially; I mean off the Earth and between the planets. There are a few really good ways, as invented by perspiring authors in science-fiction magazines. And if I miss any, which is extremely doubtful, remember that I'm writting from memory, that I hadn't read *all* the scientifiction magazines from 1926 and on, and that I am not going to go researching through the tremendous stacks of old scientifiction magazines that I now have in my possession.

Now, what DO I mean by THE BEST WAYS TO GET AROUND? Briefly, by the word BEST, I mean so pseudo-logical that you could almost leave off the "pseudo". See? (No)

For instance, Jack Williamson's geodesic machinery, wherein he warps space around, appeals to me as being pure fairy tale stuff. He just gives a lot of verbal hocus-pocus, and runs off reams of litterary fertilizer until we throw up our hands in disgust and say; "O.K., O.K., Jack, to hell with that, let's get on with the 'story'. We'll grant you that you *can* get around." —And we're willing to grant E.E. Smith the same privilege. He *DOES* get around-anybody disagree? The question is; how? Oh, by useing "X", and the inertialess drive. The same with brother Burroughs. What do we care if dear old John Carter "yearns" himself to Mars? He gets there, and we are happy, or were happy.

So, we exclude all those from THE BEST WAYS TO GET AROUND. They are very nice and convenient to get people places; but, when we run across one of the "BEST WAYS" we often wonder if it REALLY WOULDN'T be possible, provided — —. Of course, that word "provided" is the catch-the reason why we really aren't going around that way.

Again-So, way back there, Edmond Hamilton, and a hundred others, have used the idea of *light-preasure* in an attempt to get away from rockets. But he didn't tell us how, scientifictionaly. In direct contrast to vauge statements made regarding the use of *light-preasure* as propulsion, I remember the MOON CONQUORS, by R.H. Romans, in a 1931 (I think) (You're right, 4SJ) quarterly. You've seen radiometers. The things with black and white vanes placed in a vacuum. The theory is that the opposite shades cause unbalanced light preasure, so that the vanes go around and around. Romans invented a pseudo-scientifically logical way to use *light-preasure*, once he got his ship in space. His scientist invented a compound of *absolute black*. (Which is also obtainable in a darkroom) A small square of darkroom-or, I mean, absolute black painted on the posterior of the ship, and regulated at will, gave the same ship quite respectable speeds. Certainly it won't work outside of a story-but, I'm talking scientifictionally. Romans used his imagination, and we all had fun.

In the same story, Romans used a swell device to get the ship off the earth. He used a mile-long tube, composed of circular magnets. It was a *magnetic gun*. Each magnet pulled the ship towards it, and then, as the ship passed it, the magnet's poles were reversed, and made to repel the ship. With each magnet at maximum charge, either pulling or pushing the ship, according to whether it was in front or behind the latter, the same erupted from the tube with the necessary 7 M.P.S. velocity of escape, and so was off on the way to the moon. What's wrong with the idea? I dunno.

John W. Campell (Jr.) used to have brainstorms: in fact, he invented *two* of THE BEST WAYS TO GET AROUND. One, in the first of the ARCOT, MOREY, and WADE stories, "PIRACY PREFERRED", was that of molecular motion. All the little molecules in a bar of metal go madly around in every possible direction. If you could invent, as Campbell did in the story, an electro-magnetic vibration that would force all the mollecules to go in the same direction, then the bar of metals would go in that direction, since it would be them. So Mr. Campbell hooked the thing up to his ship, and off he went to Venus, or some other planet. Well, it *would* work, wouldn't it, *provided* (ah yes!) you could make all the mollecules go into one directional flow.

And the other brainstorm was when Aarn Munro, in the MIGHTIEST MACHINE, decided that momentum and velocity were wave formations, and therefore, one should be able to *tune into them*! (Anyone should be able to think up a simple theory like that.) Not a bad WAY TO GET AROUND-in a science fiction story.

Back in 1930, or some such year, Charles R. Tanner wrote THE FLIGHT OF THE MERCURY, in the old WONDER STORIES. In that story he told you just how to go ahead and make an ETHERPROPELLER, provided there is such a thing as ether, and Osmium B. The theory is: you use water screws, air propellers, and so why not an ether propeller? Put a cork in motionless water. Start a wave motion in the water with your hand. If the length of the wave is greater than the diameter of the cork, the cork just bobs up and down and stays where it is. If the lengths of the waves are shorter than the diameter of the cork, the waves go around it, and the cork still stays right where it is. If the length of the wave is exactly the diameter of the cork, tho cork rides right off, in the trough of the wave, at the same speed as that of the wave formation. Now invent an electro-magnetic vibration-by useing the metal Osmium B —exactly the length of a Copper atom. Make your ship of copper, putting the ether propeller, that which causes vibration in the ether, at the end of the ship, and presto! all the copper atoms move along in the trough of the ether waves, at the same speed as the other waves, which is the speed of light. And, Mr. Tanner is off for Mars, in a super-plausibly scientifictional way.

HELL SHIP, in last year's ASTOUNDING, Arthur J. Burks put forth an idea which had been discussed by engineers before he had ever used It. They just didn't know how to do it. Mr. Burks did-didn't he write the story. At least, the idea gave him more earthly benifit than it gave the engineers. Maybe he thinks he invented it —I don't know, nor does it matter: He used it, the idea of gravatic lines of force, forming a spider web throughout the solar system. With the proper machinery, which he ascribed with good attention to detail, you could crawl up those lines of force like a spider. This idea is so plausible that it might be placed in the same catagory as rocket propulsion, which is fact.

THE MOTH, in this year's ASTOUNDING, contains another of those ideas of interplanatary locomotion which I call one of THE BEST WAYS TO GET AROUND. Don't worry, I'm not pointing to myself with pride. I just wrote the story, Charles R. Tanner conceived the idea. He tossed it off paranthetically one night, and promptly forgot about it. The idea — —If all objects are in motion, according to the Lorentz-Fitzgerald contraction theory, lose length in the direction of motion, why couldn't an artificialy produced cause instantaneous motion, why couldn't an artificialy produced contraction cause instantaneous motion, proportional to length-loss? Not a thing in the world against it, my friends, all you have to do is to find a way to cause the artificial contraction of the ship in question. Of course, in my story, I invented a force-field — —very handy when you're in a tight spot! —which caused tho electrons to flatten out. This force acted on the ship and everything within. Therefore, any speed up to a little below that of light could be obtained, and that bogey man so often ignored in scientifiction, acceleration, was disposed of at the start, since there was nothing that had a tendancy to stay behind. There is the real inertialess drive, which E.E. Smith talked of, but never used.

(Paranthetically: When Charles R. Tanner saw the story containing his idea in print, he became enthused, and promptly invented and named all machines used in the process, discovered a new and ultimate particle called the "graviton", that which makes the proton 1846 times heavier than the electron, and practically drew plans for the force field which caused the contraction. When he finished we knew exactly *how* to obtain speeds far exceding both those of Smith and Campbell. Our inventions were plausable, and they'd work, provided — —)

I've just about reached the end of the list, though there are one or two others that might be mentioned right here at the tail end of the article. Jules Verne, I suppose, has to be credited with the first ship fired from a canon, in ONCE AROUND THE MOON. Wells takes the bow for gravity plates, which Willy Ley so neatly disposed of, only he called it "cavorite" in THE FIRST MEN IN THE MOON., and Roy Cummings used it effectivly in AROUND THE UNIVERSE (and a hundred others). In a story in the old WONDER Donald Wolheim put his rocket ship on a huge wheel, rotated the wheel and flung it off into space. Fair, except that the acceleration would be killing.

AND THAT'S ABSOLUTLY ALL THE BEST WAYS TO GET AROUND. Unless there are some of those which I haven't heard of. If you know of some, I would like to be enlightened.

—ROSS ROCKYLYN

"I suppose you've heard about what happened to my brother Jerry?" Ray Spencer asked me; I shook my head. "The whole family was worried about him for a while: couldn't tell whether he had sleeping-sickness, or what. All we knew was that he'd gone coma listening to some phonograph records when he was alone in the house. Perhaps the intense emotional effect of the music, plus its stentor, was the cause.

"When I returned home, he lay cold on the floor in front of the radio-phonograph. The automatic release had shut off the record, but the current was still on, and the volume dial was turned full strength. Nothing I could do would rouse my brother, so-scared —I put him to bed and called a doctor, who had him taken to a hospital for observation. No one could determine what was the trouble, and since we couldn't afford to keep him at the hospital indefinitely, we brought Jerry back home. And although it wasn't exactly appropriate, I couldn't help remembering the story of the Sleeping Beauty whenever I looked into his room and saw him, apparently only napping.

"Then one day I heard him-still in his trance-whisperingly singing. The indistinct notes were reminiscent of one of Chaikovsky's ballet pieces. I tried vainly to wake him. He sighed on and on until the faint breath of a voice softened into silence....

"When at last he did awake, I had been listening to some continental communiques in the adjoining room, with the door open so that I could look in on him in case of emergency. The program ended and was followed by concert music. I don't care much for symphony, so I arose and went to the radio to switch it off. At the same time, Jerry stirred: I heard his bed creak. Turning to look his way, I twisted the wrong dial, and the music thundered: my brother began to toss on his bed. Disregarding the racket for a moment in excitement at seeing him move, I ran in to him, shouting, shaking him a little. His hands groped, found mine, and clung to them. Painfully he endeavored to raise himself, dropped back perspiring and panting. Then he screamed-horribly! —as if all Hell's devils were shovelling all Hell's coals on him, and opened his eyes, his face taut with dread. He recognized me. In a moment I had soothed him back to normalcy. He was perfectly all right from then on.

"Or at least we thought so. But since you're so interested in metaphysics, get him to tell you about the vision he had during his catalepsy. He won't feel embarrassed; he's told it to others. Just say that I mentioned it to you." Ray had finished. Later, when I chanced upon Jerry Spencer, I brot him up to my apartment for dinner. The meal over, he smiled at my query concerning his comatose dream, and related:

"None in my family are as interested in music as I: my belief is that to realize its full magic you must leave off talking-better still, listen to it alone-and, closing your eyes, open your mind to it. Relax-forget yourself. All of my folks poke fun at me when I sit on the floor by the radio during the concert broadcasts, my ears close to the speaker. But that is the only way by which I can really enjoy music. The very loudness, blasting at my hearing, emphasizes the tone-magic, overwhelming everything else. And sometimes, if my eyes are shut, I can see fantastic dream worlds, fiery pageants inspired by thundrous harmonies.

"I had never dared to turn on the amplifier as loud as I'd have wished. My family said that it would annoy the neighbors. So that day when I was alone at home, I thot that then was my chance, if ever, and proceeded to play my favorite record; the first scene of Chaikovsky's SWAN LAKE ballet, as loudly as possible. The sound was not so deafening as-maddening, or better still, intoxicating. How I Loved it! I sat cross-legged, eyes shut, dreaming, at last absolutely happy. More: ecstatic.

"The first notes were like an invitation emanating from a lost dimension, calling me, wheedling. Promising haven, peace. The call of the unknown: not the lure of dashing adventure but of mystery, mournful sorcery, epic splendors....

"Deep in my heart there's a sort of innate Slavic sadness which responded to the music's plaint, and my thought traveled with the melody effortlessly on and on. The warm darkness of my closed eyes lightened to infinities of cold, deep-blue emptiness, through which I felt myself gliding as the theme progressed.

"Each harmonic burst, every wailing echo, dominated me. My thought was borne farther and farther like a leaf in a tempest.... There were base chords which made my throat quiver, and tears burned under my lowered eyelids. I felt a tingling at my shoulders, and with eyes still closed but discerning by a sort of dream-vision, I half-consciously turned, beheld luminous yellow-draperies? —fluttering behind me, bouying me: like scarf-wings, whipping comet-tails.

"An instinctive transient fright gripped me, admonishing me to withdraw from this blue region into the calid darkness from which I had come-but the melody's urge was stronger than my feeble urge to retreat. The azure became flecked with diamond points of light which augmented into great white moons, and from one to another in a vast network rayed pulsing filaments, vascular channels of fluid light.

"A stupendous chorus of clear unhuman voices, as from diamond throats, emanated from these linked moons, of which the music which had conveyed me was only a distorted, ghostly echo....In tangible waves this greater music rippled around the webbed moons, beating against me as though to force me away on its tides I know not whither.

"Beneath me was a limitless tract of grey slime which rose and fell torpidly as with the breathing of a somnolent subterranean thing. The moonlight burned brightly on it, and crawling across it from some remote place came-trees? —snaky-rooted things whose prehensile branches bore, instead of leaves, flexible lenses.... They left behind them red trails on the slime, and excrementory ribbons of thin blue vapor streamed from their topmost appendages. Occasionally they paused to feed, focussing their lenses upon the gelatinous ground, which became luminously white under the concentrated light. The sucking mouths of the serpentine roots absorbed this matter, and red viscosity seeped into the eaten places, greying rapidly under the moon's effulgence, chemically affected by it.

"And the trees mated. Gynandrous, they converged in pairs or groups, pressing close together, thrusting their limbs into one enormous cluster, aggregating their lenses into a series of complex, compact forms ...shuddering with a violent ardor....From erectile protuberances rimming the lenses ruby liquid spurted, bursting with incandescence under the condensed moonlight.

"Spent, drooping, the trees separated, and the radiant orgasmic matter drifted lightly down to the slime, burning fitfully as the trees moved away indifferently.

"Apparently these flickering radiances fed, for gradually they grew, dulling, becoming opaque, substantial — —thrusting out probing roots, developing limbs, wandering like their parents. They snailed onward out of sight, all of them.

"Silently, a phosphorescent green river raced like a bolt of furcate lightning over the green wastes. It was composed not of water but of myriad tiny luminous crawling insects. A conscious river, altering its tortuous course at will, small streams deviating from the main body and meandering erratically, then rejoining the general current. This river's end drew into sight, flashed under me and into the distance, leaving fast-greying red paths on the slime.

"The moon's music assailed me; simultaneously I felt those man-measures, which had carried me so long, cease, leaving me without a link to my own world-helpless against the inexorable tide of the lunar melody, which, bursting more loudly, swept me higher, through an interstice of the circulatory web, into blue infinity. And there it left me; fading ripples of it would lap me, but were too dissapated then to sweep me farther.

"I floated aimlessly in the void, it seemed for ages, less a body than a mind, aware of neither hunger nor thirst nor ill of any sort other than a dreadful sapping weariness.

"There was no way of reckoning time, but after an eternity of loneliness and self-boredom, I heard a glissando of mellow tintinabulations. A troop of small stars flashed toward me like a scattered handful of sparkling white gems, whirling in interweaving dance of enchantment, tinkling glad clear tunes like the babbling of crystal brooks. The joyous, youthful essence of their song so charmed me that I forgot my weariness and vocally ventured to imitate it.

"At last they broke their circle and swept away, single-file, out of sight, diminishing with distance.

"For awhile I hummed their song, but with every repetition it lost some of its starry quality and gained a human-ness, earthiness, animalism-until it impressed me no longer beautiful, and I was silent....Wearily the sluggish ages passed ...in the illimitable blue solitudes....

"Eventually I heard the man-music, again like a summons-its vibrations piercing the moon-net, receding, drawing me with it. Its power increased with every unit of retregression, dragging me with it. Over the wastes of slime it dragged me, all in a fraction of seconds. Wind tore at me, racketing in my ears, drowning music of both moons and man.

"In a flash of cataclysm, of cosmic pandemonium, the moons, jostled out of their places by my abrupt passage through the web, strained apart, snapping their pulsant filamental arteries. White, searing drops of blood of light oozed from the severed ducts, hissing as they fell, and splashed on the slime, which heaved torturedly. The crawling trees reared upon their writhing roots, flailing their lensed limbs, and the phosphorescent rivers halted suddenly, piling into swiftly disintegrating mounds.

"The rain of light blood thinned and ceased: the moons dimmed and plunged earthward, lusterless. As they touched the tempestuously tossing slime, it shrieked stridently, deafeningly —*cosmically*! An outcry voicing all life's inherent dread of the horror of pain and death, which arose from all sides, like an auditory vise, tightening upon and crushing me. The blue chaos was wiped away by utter blackness; the shriek weakened, ceased.

"I opened my eyes, shut them-dazzled by daylight, and opened them again, but cautiously. My brother Ray was standing over me, shaking me, calling my name ...AND IT WAS I WHO HAD SCREAMED!"

As I Remember ——

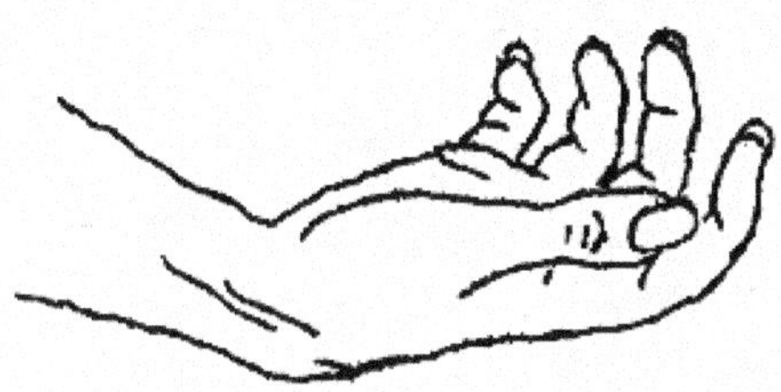

As I remember, August Derleth wrote, a time back: "My personal favorite of the Lovecraft stories is THE RATS IN THE WALL, followed by DUNWICH HORROR, COLOUR OUT OF SPACE, THE OUTSIDER, WHISPERER IN DARKNESS." H.P.L. liked MUSIC OF ERICH ZANN as well as anything he did, COLOUR next. Donald Wandrei is busy in St. Paul writing plays and shorts. "My average day brings me anywhere from ten to fifty letters that must be answered."

As I remember one night in Coney Island found seven strange looking fellows, fans and authors, crowded into a car for a posed picture. Ross Rocklynne, freshly freckled by a New Yawk sun, at the steering wheel, Jack Agnew at his side with Mark (I'm makin' my mark in pulps) Reinsburg and immediately in back of Rocklynne a fellow with too much hair, a tan that would make an Ethiopian blush, and teeth, Bradbury, augmented by the humorously verbose Erle Korshak, the professorly nice Bob Madle and one V. Kidwell. I recall also a night at Mort Weisinger's home during July with Rocklynne, Ackerman, Morojo, Hornig, Binder, Schwartz, Darrow and again Bradbury. A picture was taken that night and the only ones with decent smiles were Ackerman and the under-done personality who edits this magazine. Hornig looked strangely thoughtful with his hand to his chin, Mort had a cigarette drooping from his lip and Darrow, Schwartz and Binder all were lost in profound contemplation of the little birdie which Mort's brother held. I remember also a night on Central Park, a stag night, when it was raining convulsively and Binder, Bradbury, Hornig, Rocklynne and Darrow all clambered into a rocking boat and swished out onto the glittering water, yodeling popular tunes at the way-way top of their corny contraltos. Binder has a pleasing bath-tub baritone, while Hornig can imitate a frog at the drop of a body. Darrow was strangely silent, but that man Bradbury and Rocklynne set up such a howl that the Park authorities came out in a submarine, thinking that the Loch Ness monster had turned up again. This was all settled when someone pulled the plug and everyone drowned peacefully.

Going way back in the cobwebs I seem to recall a letter arriving at an Eastern post-office addressed to Mars. It was returned marked: Insufficient Postage.

As I remember Charlie Hornig wrote, on January 9th: "On Tuesday, February 20th, 1940, I'll be in Los Angeles. I will write for Futuria Fantasia, but my rates are 12 cents a word, before acceptance. I haven't seen GONE WITH THE WIND yet, but if I stop off to see it on the road, expect me two days later than heretofore planned. If I walk it, expect me at the city limits on the R car-line, Whittier, the same time of the morning, only about 18 months later. I'll bring my overcoat and shovel along for the annual sun showers and orange blizzards." And later, from Hornig: "I liked the latest issue of Futuria Fantasia very much, especially the page of conventional descriptions over which I laughed myself sick and silly. The note about Bradbury and the mask and the blonde in the Paramount is the funniest thing I've ever read in a fan-mag."

I seem to remember being at someone's house not so long ago and glancing thru a thick manuscript under submission to John W. Campbell. I seen to remember that the author was

Robert A. Heinlein, member of our LaSfl. And the other day that story popped up in Astounding as a Nova, "IF THIS GOES ON —" And it seems to me that here and now Bob should take a bow for a swell story. And thanks to Campbell for providing it with a Rogers cover and Rogers interiors. OMEGA — —

www.ingramcontent.com/pod-product-compliance
Lightning Source LLC
LaVergne TN
LVHW050658200726
843506LV00010B/1571